# Buddy's Tail

A Novel by K. Anne Russell

Ages 9 and up.

What reviewers are saying --

The well-developed plot is written to delight both adults and children.

**— Pat McGrath Avery, Foreword Clarion**

Each canine character is distinct, and Russell doesn't settle for hackneyed descriptions or still action scenes. Her writing is bright and intricate, fun and profound. ... A welcome addition to the canine canon for young readers.

**— Kirkus Indie**

This fanciful tale of Buddy and his buddies transports the reader immediately into a world of highly diverse and totally captivating canines...

**— Gordon Osmond, Bookpleasures**

Though *Buddy's Tail* is meant for children, it is a deeply textured novel with lessons that will outlast its reader demographic.

**— San Francisco Book Review**

This is an amazing story that will teach your children responsibility, the importance of friendship, the bond of love, free will, animal welfare, and the acceptance of death for both man and pet.

**— April Renn, MyBookAddiction**

Buddy's Tail is one of those books that touch your heart.

**— Sandra K. Stiles, The Musings of a Book Addict**

Russell has mastered the art of writing from an animal point of view and makes her story of life, camaraderie and death among dogs not only entertaining, suspenseful, sentimental and humorous, but she also manages to make some poignant points about relationships in general...

**— Grady Harp, Amazon Top 10 Reviewer**

This is a very imaginative story about a dog's adventures in life and in the afterlife.

The book ... deals with animal neglect and the responsibility of having a pet - lessons a child should learn.

This book teaches responsibility. I HIGHLY recommend this book.

The story takes place in the Southwest with vivid descriptions that bring the locales alive. The writing is crisp, entertaining, and thankfully devoid of the clichés and platitudes that sometimes plague new authors.

This is a story based on the love of dogs for their human partners and the role they play in their lives. It tugs at your heart and will be enjoyed by all animal lovers.

Buddy's Tail is a dog story that shows the great connection and love that dogs and humans have for one another.

The book is smartly written. I think it is a great learning tool to share with your child.

I loved it!!! I will be reading it to the children in my family and encouraging everyone I know to do so also.

I believe any child grades 3-6 would love to travel with Buddy and his friends as they move about their neighborhood and even Haven (doggie heaven) setting out to do only what is right.

# Contents

*This book is dedicated*
*with admiration and pride*
*to the United States Marine Corps*
*Military Working Dogs and their handlers*
*at MCAGCC Twentynine Palms, California,*
*whose efforts were an inspiration*
*to me while writing this book,*
*and to my beloved Buddy,*
*because I know you*
*will come for me.*

# Chapter 1

Buddy Boutonniere was not the sort of dog you'd expect to find in our neighborhood, and that's a fact. In Yucca Dunes, tastes in canines ran to Chihuahuas, American Pit Bull Terriers and the occasional Rottweiler. I'm a Border Collie, a bit of a standout myself, but I had an important job at a local golf course, so I belonged.

Buddy was a poodle, and not just any piddly-diddly little poodle. He was a Standard Poodle, white as the snow on Mount San Jacinto and tall as its craggy peaks. Yep, he was one long cool drink of milk. He had a frizzy hairdo, ears as big as window curtains, a nose broad enough for roadrunner landings and the silliest tail you ever saw. It looked like a cross between spun cotton candy and a tumbleweed.

We poked good natured fun at him every chance we got, Javier and I. Javier was my Chihuahua pal, who considered himself some kind of Hispanic cultural hero, the Zorro of the back alleys. That little guy had a crusader's heart in a chili pepper package. Truth is he was so short and skinny, Javier had trouble casting a shadow. He was always afraid of being squashed by some two-legged dude in cross-trainers the size of skateboards, so he hung with me for protection when he managed to escape from his home.

Guess I should introduce myself. I'm MacKenzie. That's a first-class name for a female herding dog. Javier always said I never got it out of my blood. Even after I retired from the golf gig, I couldn't help myself, always wanting to look after folks and guide

1

them in the right direction. Buddy's situation sure brought out the mother in me.

Javier and I stopped by Buddy's place nearly every day. Buddy was dealt a bad hand in the human department. His people were clueless about our kind. Warren and Lulu Swindell got him for their daughter, Brianna, who went off to college without so much as a hi-dee-ho. The parents didn't realize Buddy would get so big. HellllOOOOOOO! Anyway, they exiled Buddy to the yard, where he made do with a lean-to for shelter from the desert sun and a stunted jacaranda tree for scenery. I preferred my life on the street to the prison he called home.

My *pequeño* pal and I visited frequently, because Bud's people were not only stupid and unfeeling, they were negligent. Had a habit of going away for days and forgetting to leave enough food and water. We made a point of checking on Buddy, because if they had left him short again, I could pick up a snack for him from the trashcans behind McDonald's up on Palm Tree Street. Thing that got me was that Buddy never complained. He took what life threw at him. Believe me, it wasn't much, but he always had a smile and a kind word. He had a disposition as sweet as desert flowers after a flash rain and a heart as big as the Mojave.

I'm going to tell you Buddy's story. I witnessed most of it first-hand, and my pals filled me in on the rest. It's a roller coaster of a tale, with more twists and turns than a jackrabbit chase down the arroyo. I guess it's my story too. I was one smug sister. I thought I knew how things were, but that peach of a pooch turned my canine cosmos on its ear.

Those dunderheads the Swindells did get one thing right though—his name. Buddy Boutonniere. Buddy was just the sort of mellow guy who would go through life with a blossom in his buttonhole, if he'd had a button hole. That's why it's so strange he turned out to be the one who broke the biggest rule of all.

# Chapter 2

That Tuesday in May was a typical visit. I remember it like it was yesterday. Javier was wearing his fancy green and red collar.

"It's for Cinco de Mayo. Don't you guys know anything?" Javier shrugged first one, then the other shoulder, so his nametag hung properly.

Buddy poked his nose between the bars of the gate to the Swindell backyard. "It looks very nice on you. I wish I had a colored collar."

"Yeah, Bud, what were they thinking, giving you that matte black? Yuck! I see you in peacock blue." Javier, whose coat was the color of sand dunes at daybreak, took great pride in his appearance.

Sometimes I got impatient with these two. "Would you guys give it a rest with the fashion report? Here, Bud." I shoved a bag of fries through the bars. "I picked these up for you on the way over. When was the last time you ate?"

"Thanks, Mac." Buddy sniffed the wrapper, his big nostrils flaring in appreciation. He selected some fries and chewed, his eyes closing. After a swallow and a smack of ebony lips, he answered. "Ummmm, these are wonderful. I stretched out what they left for me, but I ran short yesterday morning."

"I know how you like your *frites, mon ami*." I never forgot they were his favorite.

"We gotta get him some *carne asada*. After that, he will spit on those fries." Javier waltzed over and leaned on the bars.

"I'm sure I would like that, too. I loved the tacos you brought."

"Javier insisted I stop at Taco Bell. He can't carry much himself." I tried to see around Buddy into the backyard where the water bowl was. If it was empty, he would be forced to drink pool water, which wasn't good for him.

"Hey, just because I couldn't manage the Burrito Supreme, you don't have to be acting all *grande muchacha*."

"No offense intended." I nosed Javier gently on the top of his head.

Buddy shook the last of the fries on the ground. One bounced toward the wall, and he walked over to retrieve it. I got a full view of the empty bowl, and my hackles rose. "Buddy, why don't you go on a barking jag? Bother the neighbors so they call Animal Control."

"*Si*, your people are being cruel to you, man." Javier bounced up on his little legs, looking for all the world like he was going to get in the ring with somebody.

"I couldn't do that. They're just forgetful. Brianna was very kind."

"Brianna's history. Gone off to college, Bud." In my opinion, he needed to stop making excuses for them. "You're left with the two duds she has for parents."

"They'll be home soon and will fill my dish."

"I think this is one case where you're justified in biting the hand that feeds you." His brow wrinkled in a furious knot, Javier nodded toward the empty container.

"There are dogs starving all over this valley. I am thankful for the home I have and loyal to my humans." Buddy finished the last of the potatoes, licked the wrapper, and tucked the paper under his dish so it couldn't blow into the pool. "Thank you for the treat, Mac. It was scrumptious."

"I'll be back later with something for your dinner."

"I wish I could do something for you." Buddy leaned his forehead on the bars of the locked gate.

"You can, *muchacho*. Howl your head off, so we can have ringside seats when they come to give *Señor* Swindell a citation." Javier was dancing now, his nails tapping on the concrete. "We'd love to see that come down, man."

"Cool it, Salsa King," I said. "Buddy doesn't like to make waves."

"I don't have your hot Latin blood." Buddy winked at Javier.

"You got a warm heart, big guy. That much I know." Javier squeezed through the bars, waited for Buddy to lean his big head down, and licked him on the chin. Those big poodle ears folded down around Javier like a matador's cape.

# Chapter 3

Later that night, I brought Buddy the remains of a Big Mac, but the next day Javier and I didn't get over to his place until mid-afternoon. A car sat in the driveway, and a stake with a sign on it jutted out of the front lawn.

I greeted Buddy with a lick on the cheek. "When did that turn up?"

"This morning. A man came with it in his trunk. What does it mean?"

"I know what it means." Javier strutted over to the stake and peed on it. "They put one of those up next door. Next thing we knew, the people who lived there went away and new people moved in. I still miss the little girl from the first family. She used to rub my belly."

"Oh, my." Buddy's gaze fell to his paws. His front legs were straight up and down like palm trunks. "I wonder where we could be going. How will you find me?"

"If you're in this valley, pal, I'll find you." My voice sounded more confident than I felt.

Javier passed through the fence bars and surveyed Buddy's yard. Except for the pool and a bench in need of some varnish, it was little more than a cement box. "Let's not panic yet, *amigo*. Perhaps they will not be successful in finding others to take their place. This is not very attractive, to dogs or people."

I was trying to think of something reassuring to say to Buddy when I heard it. I was halfway across the yard and picking up speed before Javier figured out what was happening.

"Mac, stop! You could get hurt." Javier shot back through the gate, his voice rising to a shrill squeak.

Buddy gasped and banged into the bars as if he could part them. "It's the Hummer! No, MacKenzie, don't chase it."

I heard them. They were far away, like the voice of my conscience, but I could no more stop than I could change the color of my fur. I hated that Hummer. I hated its metallic growl and the smelly gray streaks its left on the road when it turned. Most of all I hated the man who drove the moving black mountain.

I fell in behind the beast as it cruised past Buddy's house. The harsh sounds blaring from its windows fueled my anger. Barks flew from my throat like summer thunder. The thing picked up speed and sailed away from me, smoke spewing out of its tail like the beginning of a brush fire.

Panting, I trotted to a halt at the next street, the taste of oil fouling my tongue. Someday, I would catch that evil man and get even for Howie.

I returned to Buddy's place in time to see his humans packing their car with suitcases. Javier had curled himself up in Buddy's shadow, and the two watched as Warren Swindell eased his paunch behind the wheel and closed the dusty station wagon's door.

I collapsed on the walk, my panting more under control, as the car backed into the street.

"*Carumba*, they could have waved at you, Bud." Javier shook his head and stretched.

"They filled my bowls, and I got table scraps at lunchtime."

"Big of 'em." Javier leaned over Buddy's food dish and sniffed. His nostrils wrinkled as if he were smelling road kill.

Buddy changed the subject, sliding his paw through the bars until it touched my hind foot. "Mac, I know you hate that

Hummer, but you must be more careful. It is a contest you cannot win. Howie would not want you to be taking such risks."

"We'll see." I sat up, perked my ears and a ring of fire gripped my heart. I could just detect the growl of the wicked thing in the distance as it sped through our neighborhood.

# Chapter 4

In the weeks to come, Buddy's life changed for the better. The boredom he endured at the Swindell homestead was broken by a parade of humans. People arrived in groups of two or three, toured the house, examined the yard, craned their necks to study the roof and the chimney of the trim little house, and returned to their cars chattering like crows on a newly mown lawn.

Javier pumped Buddy for details about the visitors, mostly about their shoes. The bigger the shoes, the wider Javier's eyes got as Buddy described the visitors, until I was sure they would pop out and roll into the rose bed.

Buddy was happy to share his news even though we realized that the tours would end and he would have to go away someday. But Buddy never had news before, so it was sweet to have the tables turned and be listeners for a change.

That Saturday, we were late. Javier was caught sneaking out through the open garage by Papa Borrego. He was stuck in the house until the Borrego family's youngest, little Juanita, left the front door ajar when she crossed the lawn to check the mailbox.

When Buddy saw us coming down the street, he jumped up, danced a few steps forward and draped his paws over the top rung of the gate, his sail-like ears swinging in the breeze.

"You look ready to burst, man." Javier pranced through the bars under Buddy's rangy torso, so smug about his escape from Juanita that he didn't shy away from Bud's big feet for once.

11

"I have had the most wonderful day." Buddy sprang to the ground, flung himself in front of us, crossed his legs and broke into a silly grin.

"We're all ears." Javier shot his up to their full three-inch height.

"A lady came. No, let me back up and start at the beginning."

"Was the man with the gunboats here?" Javier tucked his hind legs under and shuttered.

"Yes, he was here. He's always along, with a big pile of papers stuffed under his arm, talking as fast as a pigeon in mating season." Buddy winked his gravy-colored eyes.

"Oh, man, his feet are huge." Javier grimaced, eyes closed, his front paws shaking.

"Snap out of it, Javier. Buddy, about the lady?"

"Actually, there were three ladies. The two younger ones stuck with the talky man."

"Bigfoot!"

"Javier, chill!" I sidled next to Javier and stroked his cheek with my muzzle to calm him. "Buddy, get on about the women."

"I'm getting to the good part. The older lady didn't seem interested in the house. She came outside and sat on the bench by the pool."

"So?" Javier's voice was back in its normal range.

"Except for the pool man, people hardly ever come into my yard. And nobody sits." Buddy shot up onto his haunches. "Then she motioned for me to come to her."

"What did you do?"

"I obeyed. She patted my head. Not like Mr. Swindell. He bonks me and flattens my topknot." Buddy's eyes went out of focus, his head swaying from side to side as he recollected. "She rubbed under my ears. Stroked my cheeks. I don't think I've ever felt anything so good."

"Did she do it right here?" Javier was pointing to the special place on his own ear. I could not remember the last time I'd had my ear stroked the way Buddy described. A wave of sadness swept over me.

"Yes, that's it, but there's more." Buddy was up now, pacing. "She patted next to her on the bench. I didn't know what to make of that at first. Then I had an inspiration. I jumped up and sat next to her."

"Whoa!" Javier's eyebrows arched, sharp as tortilla chips. "I'm not allowed on the furniture. That was a risky move."

"Her hair was gray, you know, like the hairs above Howie's eyes. Her eyes were green like new shoots of grass, and she didn't look through me. She looked right into my eyes. It was something."

"How long did she stay?" I asked.

"I can't rightly say. I lost track of time. When the others came for her, she had her arm around my shoulders and was scratching my side." Buddy blinked, a tear glistening on his lash.

"Some people are good like that. *Mamacita* Borrego, when she is not so busy with the cooking and the cleaning, sits with me sometimes. She cradles me in her apron."

I thought of Jamie, my first handler at the golf course. Jamie knew how a dog wants to be treated. We were a pair. Everyone said so. I would race along the fairway faster than the breeze, Jamie following me in the cart. I could chase geese off the fairway all day long for that man. We were inseparable until he broke his leg. Then Kurtz came.

I swallowed hard and tried to recall Jamie's face. It would not come. Only his salty scent and the firm touch of his palm on my head.

"Maybe she will buy the house," I said. My voice cracked a little, but my friends didn't notice.

"That would be wonderful. If Mr. Swindell would let me stay." Buddy spun around, his silly tail bouncing.

"Speaking of the Swindell *hombre*," Javier nodded to the driveway.

As the car pulled up, I sent a little prayer heavenward that Buddy's wish would be granted.

# Chapter 5

 I sunned myself after bathing in the runoff from the sprinklers at the new subdivision. The days were getting hotter, and I had to cool off after all the exertion. I found the Hummer in the strip mall where the McDonald's was located and gave chase. Memories of Howie's end made my blood run hot as chipotle. I did not abandon my pursuit until the evil one gunned down the onramp to Interstate 10. I was arranging my still damp fur when Javier tore across the intersection and slid into me on the wet concrete.

"Something has happened at Buddy's." He managed to spit the words out between pants.

"What's up?" I stood and shook the rest of my coat into place.

"The sign's gone. You know what that means?" Javier's spring-loaded tail vibrated.

"Tell me."

"It means the exchange of humans is about to happen."

"And that means we are about to learn what is going to happen to Buddy. Let's get over there." I set off at a slow trot so Javier could keep up.

Buddy was not at the gate when we arrived. The Swindell's car and another vehicle filled the driveway, and a third car parked behind them in the street. Javier slipped through the bars to go and find our friend, and I waited, staring at the gash in the lawn where the sign had been. The earth was disturbed like a freshly dug grave., and a worm fought to bury itself out of sight before a bird noticed it.

15

Before my pals reappeared, a man and woman, each carrying a stack of papers, left the house and walked to the driveway. They shook hands and headed to their respective cars. They both had pulled away by the time Javier and Buddy reached the gate.

The muscles over Buddy's eyes were pinched and his lip hunched to one side.

"What are you puzzling over?" I slouched against the wall in a patch of shade.

Javier passed through the bars to my side. "We watched the people through the picture window. The woman kept pointing at Buddy."

Buddy took up his usual position behind the gate. "Mr. Swindell shook his head over and over."

"Which way?"

"Like this." Javier did the "no" shake, jiggling his name tag.

Buddy sighed. "She is one of the women who came with my lady, the one who sat on the bench and looked into my eyes."

"She must have asked for you, man. That's what it means." Javier sat, his little tail rotating like a propeller.

"And Mr. Swindell refused." Buddy hung his head. "Why would he do that? I know he doesn't want me."

Try as we might we could not shed any light on the scene Buddy had witnessed. The sun moved to our side of the wall, bathing us with warmth. My morning chase caught up with me, I stretched out on the soft lawn and slipped into a welcome nap. I dreamed of Howie in the happy times. We played in the park, dodging around the statues. Sometimes, I let him win the race to the hotdog stand at the baseball diamond, where the vender gave us broken rolls smeared with generous squirts of catsup.

Startled awake by the sound of the garage door, I lifted my head in time to see Mr. Swindell's rear back into view as he dragged something out to the driveway.

16

"Buddy, is that yours? It's the biggest carrier I've ever seen." Javier was rubbing his eyes. "That would be a condominium for a guy my size."

Mr. Swindell returned to the garage and came out again carrying two bowls and a leash. He placed the bowls on top of the carrier, walked to the street, and shaded his eyes as he looked down toward the Palm Tree Street intersection.

"I'm not scheduled for a grooming." Buddy's voice trembled.

Mr. Swindell waved with his free hand. A white SUV slowed and turned into the driveway.

As a man and woman got out of the SUV, Swindell headed for us.

"Beat it, pint size," he said to Javier who sat frozen like a statue in the middle of the walkway. My friend ricocheted away from the approaching feet and cowered beneath an hibiscus bush.

"I don't like the look of this." I stood my ground.

Swindell unlocked the gate, attached the leash to Buddy's collar, and led him toward the carrier.

Buddy turned his stricken face to me. "This is it. I'll never see you again. There's no time to say the things I wanted to say."

"Be brave, Bud. I won't let you out of my sight. I'll chase the car."

The door of the carrier closed on him and the two men lifted it toward the rear of the SUV.

Buddy fought to remain standing as he was lifted, but he lost his balance and fell, his face jammed against the wire mesh. The men cursed at him to be still and strained to guide the big cage home.

The last glimpse I had of my friend was of that proud puff of a tail smashed against the bars of the crate before the woman slammed the hatch closed.

"Look, Javier, there's the answer to the mystery." Javier peered out from under a red hibiscus blossom in the direction I indicated.

As we watched, the stranger counted bills into Mr. Swindell's palm. When he was done, Swindell handed him an envelope with the silhouette of a dog in one corner.

Javier's eye narrowed to slits. His voice came in a hiss. "So, *Señor* Swindell did not want to give Buddy away to someone who would love him, he wanted to sell him to the highest bidder."

The SUV backed down the driveway.

"Go to your house and wait for me, Javier. I'm going to follow Buddy's trail."

"May your paws become wings, *amiga*."

# Chapter 6

"Oh, man, didn't you know you weren't supposed to do that?" Javier shook his head in disbelief.

"How was I supposed to know? I've never been allowed inside." Buddy sank to the ground and hid his face with his paws.

"So you were sent back here in disgrace." I dropped the bag with the Quarter Pounder I had brought as a welcome home present.

"He peed on the upholstery, man. And pooped on the carpet. I'll bet those people were steamed. Phew." Javier grinned.

"They yelled at me. I was scared. Confused. The man dragged me to the kitchen door by my ear."

"Ouch. That had to hurt," I said. Kurtz had been an ear puller.

"In more ways than one." Buddy's eyes were tearing up.

"Bad response, but you had to expect some payback, man," Javier said. "Humans are nutty about their stuff."

"Lay off, Javier. Bud didn't know. Now he does. Big deal." I shoved my offering through the bars. "Welcome back, big guy."

"Yeah, yeah. I was just poking a little fun." Javier slithered through the bars and rubbed himself against Buddy's leg. "Ah, this is good. The three *amigos* are together again."

"It's a happy day." Buddy smiled and put his paw around our tiny pal.

"Well, you can bet there is one *hombre* who is not so happy."

"Who might that be?" I said, waging my tail to generate a breeze against the sultry day.

"*Señor* Swindell. He must have had to pay the money back."

We laughed and rolled on the grass, our legs waving like banners. At least Javier and I did. There was no grass on Buddy's side, but he rolled upside down and propped his spindly legs against the fence, his ears flapping inside out.

"Yips! It's him." Javier spun upright, a grimace of fear disfiguring his mug.

"What's wrong, little fellow?" Buddy struggled up.

"It's the cable guy. I gotta split. That man's boots are the size of doormats."

"Hey, wait!" I called, too late.

Javier's backside disappeared around the ficus hedge, his hind feet a blur.

A man carrying a toolbox rounded the corner. After a wary look at us, he knelt by a cord that jutted from Buddy's house and fiddled with the metal bit that joined it to the building.

"Those are big feet." Buddy strained to get a better view between the bars.

"When you are Javier's size, everything looks like a boulder. It's nice to be bigger."

"Yes. Of course, Howie was big. With that wide retriever chest. Size didn't save him though. His arthritis slowed him down." Buddy rested the bones of his elegant nose on the bars, his generous nostrils arching to capture the workman's scent.

"His arthritis didn't kill him. The evil one did." I felt a wave of impatience with Buddy's kindness. If he met the devil himself, he would be polite, sit up and offer a paw.

"But if his joints didn't ache so much he might have made it to the curb."

I saw the scene again, just as I did in my nightmares, the slow replay, with the soundtrack of my anguished and useless barks of warning. "The Hummer wasn't slowing, Buddy, it was speeding up."

# Chapter 7

Buddy's owner was nothing if not persistent. Warren Swindell managed to resell our friend within the week. I was across town calling on an old chum over Rojo Canyon way and missed all the excitement. Fortunately, for us, Javier had given Juanita the slip and was sashaying down Buddy's street when the deal went down.

With legs like popsicle sticks, Javier was in no position to give chase, but that Chihuahua is one observant dog. He described the vehicle to me and took me to the intersection where it had left him in the dust. The car's scent was thick on the pavement.

I put my nose to the ground and got to work. Observant Javier provided me with one very important piece of information. He said the van had a red circle on the bumper. My former place of employment, the Rancho Vista Country Club used red stickers to identify member's cars. I followed Buddy's smell to the club and entered the gated grounds through the delivery entrance.

Even though I knew that golf course like the back of my paw, it took me a while to locate the house where my friend had been taken. I had to be extra careful not to run into Kurtz, the course superintendent. Let's just say Kurtzie and I did not part on good terms the last time we saw each other.

"Psst, Bud, over here." I crawled under a bush and smirked at my pal.

"MacKenzie, you found me!" Buddy loped toward me, but was pulled up short by the chain that tethered him to a pillar next to the barbeque. "Wow, you're good."

"Won't deny it. So how are the new people?"

"They seem okay. Come over here and look at this place. It's huge. I have my own room off the kitchen."

"I'll stay down here if you don't mind. This is where I worked and I don't want to run into my old boss." I peered at the fancy room beyond the tinted windows. "Looks like you've come up in the world. Don't forget about the peeing though."

"I won't. I know that now."

"I wouldn't lift my leg to those outdoor sofas either, if I were you."

Buddy got as close to me as he could, lowered his torso and legs onto the patio tiles and studied the vista beyond the low wall. "It is very beautiful here."

"It is the most spectacular golf course in the valley." I still felt the pride of working to keep the course free of those coots, mallards, and geese who carelessly pooped on the greens.

"Still, I so hoped for the green-eyed lady." Buddy hung his great head.

We sat in companionable silence, listening to the songbirds high up in the date palms and the whir of a hummingbird's wings as she journeyed among the gardenia blossoms. I started to drift off when I heard the low purr of a golf cart, followed by voices and the thwack of a ball as it was struck.

My head shot up off my paws. "Bud, you might have a great situation here, but if you want out, I can tell you how."

"I should be grateful. I realize that." Buddy sat up. "But if I could go to live with the lady, I would be the happiest dog in the world. We were meant to be together."

I sat up, too. I had to make him understand the chance he would be taking. "You realize Swindell might get so mad, he sends you to the pound. You don't have a lot of control here."

Bud's lip quivered and he pressed his paws together as if he were at attention. "You're saying I could trade a good situation for nothing."

"Worse than nothing, kid." I gave him the sternest look I could muster. "So I want you to think about it long and hard before you do anything. Give the new people a chance. Weigh your options. Promise me."

"I promise, Mac."

"Okay." Hoping I was doing the right thing, I crawled on my stomach to the low wall and raised my head so that I could see the fairway. "See those people wearing the funny clothes riding in the funny car?"

"Yes, I've wondered about them."

"Now, watch." I waited for the golfer who was about to hit bring his club back over his head and begin his downswing. Then I let forth a stream of ferocious barks.

Buddy gasped in delight as the man missed his ball sending a wad of turf airborne.

I ducked down behind the wall as the foursome looked in our direction. Buddy grinned at the men, but his smile vanished when one of the golfers yelled at him.

"Why is he shouting at us?"

"Oh, something to do with my breaking his precious concentration. He'll get over it."

We waited for another foursome to get within range. "Okay, Bud, now it's your turn, but let me tell you when." I observed the four women and the position of their balls. "Yes, we'll wait until the blond one with the ponytail hits."

After her friend executed a long iron shot down the middle of the fairway, the blond woman approached her ball. She had a bad lie on the edge of a water hazard.

I watched her position her feet with her back to the water. "Get ready, Buddy, and bark when I say. As loud as you can."

The woman's club started back. "Wait for it," I whispered. The head of the club glinted in the afternoon sun as it started its descent. "Now!"

For a slim-chested guy, Buddy sure had a deep bark. He let fly with a string of bow-wows that shook the birds right out of the palms. The woman connected with the ball, but it sliced off in a crazy direction narrowly missing her companion's cart. "Good first try, you can stop now, Bud."

As we watched, the woman reeled forward, then back, her arms pin-wheeling in mad circles. "Oh, this is too, too sweet," I said.

The woman's heels slipped over the lip of the water hazard, and, squealing, she settled into the muck up to her waist.

Out of my peripheral vision I spied another cart approaching. It was the marshal's cart and my signal to split. "So, Bud, I think you get the picture. Just remember your promise."

"I will, Mac, and thank you so much. I don't know when I've had so much fun."

# Chapter 8

Buddy lasted ten days as a country club dog. He implemented my plan and, just for good measure, barked his head off during the return trip to the Swindell household. That is how we knew he was coming home. We heard him a mile away.

I was over visiting Dumb Derek on Cactus Lane. Derek is a sweet Rottweiler guy with a sad story. He had a long gig guarding a chemical dumpsite. The toxic fumes did some damage to his brain cells. He is slow and, sometimes, addled if too much information is thrown his way at one time.

"Hear that, Derek? That's Buddy's song. I would know it anywhere." I perked my ears in the direction of the noise. "Come on, walk with me."

"I don't know, Mac, I'm not supposed to leave the yard."

"Just for a quick visit." I licked his cheek and tried not to grimace. He always tasted like insect spray.

"I'm supposed to be guarding something here." Derek looked around at the neat lawn. "Can't remember what, though."

"Take a little exercise, and it'll come to you."

"Okay." Derek strolled down the walk looking back at his front door, his tongue swinging like a pendulum. "But can you bring me back? Sometimes I can't find my way."

"Sure, pal. Glad to." I took off at a brisk trot. Derek was getting thick around the waist and needed to burn off some fat.

We rounded the hedge bordering the Swindell property in time to see Mr. Swindell shove the large carrier back into the garage. He positioned the crate against the wall, kicked it twice and stormed into the house.

As the garage door screeched into place, Buddy met us at the gate, wearing a muzzle.

"Hey, Mac. Hey, Derek," he mumbled through the contraption. He could just moisten his lips with his tongue, but could not open his mouth any farther.

"Buddy, I'm sorry. I should have mentioned a muzzle as something that might happen if you implemented the plan." I nuzzled his ear.

"No problem, Mac. I accomplished part of my mission. I'm back here at square one."

"Whoa, that is one unattractive piece of hardware, Bud." Derek stared at Buddy's nose so hard his eyes crossed.

"It feels weird, too." Buddy rubbed the clasp against the gate. "Mr. Swindell put it on me the minute we got home. I didn't think he still had it."

"Can you bark at all in that thing?"

"Sure, if I really want to make noise. But if I expect to reach any volume, I have to switch to howling. Like this." Buddy threw his curly head back and uttered a mournful, high pitched yowl. It was filled with so much longing, I almost joined in, because his voice unleashed a deep yearning in my soul. I keened like that for my mother when I was taken away for training.

Derek pointed his snout skyward and harmonized with a surprising tenor. The kitchen window slammed open and Mr. Swindell's head shot out. "Shut up, you mangy pile of bones or it's the pound for you."

"Hush, guys." I melted into the shadows.

The window slammed shut, the light in the kitchen went off and the security light came on in Buddy's box of a yard. Blinking,

Derek looked from me to Buddy and back again. "What's his problem?"

"Let's just say, Buddy has pressed all his buttons. I think you should adopt a low profile for a while, Bud, until he calms down."

"If only he would call the green-eyed lady. He could wash his hands of me." Buddy slouched to the pavement.

"Humans are dense. Look at Derek's person, keeping a house full of cats. Geez." I sneezed, just thinking about them.

"Hey, I like the cats. They're company." Derek leaned on one haunch. His pads were a funny orange color from the chemicals in the yard where he used to work.

"Some company. Do you have to bow in their presence?"

"Only Sheba's." Derek's smile was sheepish.

"I knew it! Derek, you've got to make them show you some respect."

"Now I remember!" Derek bolted to his feet. "I was guarding the kitty litter. That's what I was supposed to do. She puts it out in the side garden."

"What are you talking about? No self-respecting dog guards cat poop."

"It smells as bad as the chemical drums I tended on the job." A long finger of drool dangled from the end of Derek's tongue.

Buddy and I locked eyes in mute bewilderment.

"Can you take me home now, MacKenzie? I've got to get back to work."

"Sure thing, Derek." I winked at Buddy and turned toward the street. "I'll come back later, Bud. I want to know if you met a mean guy named Kurtz over at the club."

"Does he have jowls like a bloodhound and eyes like a rattlesnake?"

"Bingo!" My old nemesis was still at Rancho Vista.

# Chapter 9

"He hit you?" I realized I was pacing back and forth in front of Buddy like a caged lion in a zoo, but I couldn't make myself stop.

"Yes, he hit me here." Buddy pointed to his left cheek. "I yelped out loud. Then he grabbed my chain and yanked it up in the air."

"The creep was trying to strangle you."

"I was taller than he realized."

"Kurtz is built like a fireplug with an eating disorder."

"When he saw that he couldn't get the chain high enough to lift my feet off the ground, he threw it at me and kicked me in the leg."

"That's Kurtz all over. Where were your new people?" I sniffed Buddy's leg at the spot where Kurtz's boot had connected. I could still detect the disgusting scent of him on Buddy's fur.

"They were out shopping. After that, I made a point of barking only when my humans were at home. I don't think he would have hit me in their presence, although he is awfully mean."

"You don't know the half of it, friend."

"Besides, they were the ones I was trying to persuade, right?"

"Right, and it worked." I sat next to the gate. "Looks like Mr. Swindell has calmed down. Your muzzle is gone."

"They are getting ready to leave again, so they had to remove it."

I would have to factor bringing food for Buddy into my activities for the near future. "You know, Bud, I don't think of myself as a vengeful person, but I've got to do something about that Kurtz."

"You're not vengeful Mac, but it is your nature to try to fix things that are wrong. You want the Hummer man brought to justice because he killed Howie."

"Exactly." Hearing the hated Hummer mentioned, I couldn't help cocking an ear to listen for the distinct rumble of its engine.

"But MacKenzie, you're not responsible for righting every wrong. You've got to take care of yourself. Sometimes, I think you're carrying the whole world on your shoulders, at least the canine part of it." Buddy poked my shoulder with his nose and licked my cheek with the velvet edge of his tongue. "You're my guardian angel."

"There are no angels, Bud. We have to protect our own."

"It isn't often I get to say this, but you're one hundred percent wrong, MacKenzie." Buddy circled, giving me a view of that ridiculous tail, and lowered himself to the pavement. "I know there are angels because some are here on earth."

"Yeah, name two."

"Easy. The green-eyed lady and you."

Dogs have many advantages over humans. One of them is you can't see us blush.

# Chapter 10

The next morning I woke with a devilish plan. It put me in such good humor I made a special trip to Ma and Pa Carpenter's Kitchen on Ramona Boulevard to score an omelet for Buddy. Their food is homemade and the portions are like mountains, so the trashcan out back brims with leftovers. I helped myself to a half-eaten portion of buckwheat pancakes drenched in butter and syrup and scored just what I was looking for, a ham and cheese three-egg beauty that had barely been touched.

My plan for dealing with Kurtz came to me in a dream. It was perfect. Why? Because its success rested on the meanness that lay at the core of the man's soul. I was sure I could land my ex boss in an embarrassing situation, and if I were lucky, get him fired from Rancho Vista.

The omelet was so heavy, my jaw ached by the time I reached Buddy's place. I dropped the greasy bag into which I had nosed the leftovers and shoved it through the bars of the gate.

"Hey, Bud! It's Mac with something special." I rested on my haunches, satisfied he would be overjoyed with what I had brought. After all, Buddy was a cheese-oholic. "Bud, you there?"

No answer.

I pressed myself against the neighbor's wall to see as much as I could of the Swindell's backyard. "Bud?"

Circling to the front of the garage, I saw that the car was not in the driveway. Although Mr. Swindell seldom put it away, he could have driven it inside to load something heavy.

I focused my ears on the house and listened. Perhaps they had finally allowed Buddy inside. Somehow, he had made it clear he had learned not to pee on the furniture. There were no sounds within the house from humans or big animals, only bugs and machines.

I returned to the gate and nosed my gift out of sight behind the wall. They must have taken him to the vet or the groomer to deal with his unruly curls. His topknot was getting out of control again. He would find the omelet when he returned and thank me tomorrow.

The golf course was an emerald carpet rippling in the midday sun. Only the tree-shaded rough glistened with water droplets. Soon the grass would begin to turn brown and the sand show through on the greens. Summer temperatures were hard on the course but fewer players would come out in the heat, so everything balanced out.

After slithering through a drainage portal in the high wall, I started my search on the sixth hole where I spotted the marshal handing moistened towels to two sweaty players. Trotting along the shady side of the cart path, I passed more players on seven and dodged around the refreshments cart on eight. The driver recognized me and waved. She used to give me snacks.

Coming out of a clutch of trees behind the tee box on nine, I saw him. Kurtz was lurking in the shadow of a jacaranda tree slumped in his dingy green work cart. On the seat next to him was his prized Pinehurst cap. I do not know what Pinehurst means, but members seemed to remark upon that hat. Kurtz's heavy face would rise up in a crooked smile that never reached his eyes. He would doff the cap, nod, and place it back on his head in a slow oily motion. He loved that thing.

I circled behind the tree and dropped to my stomach. I crawled behind the cart and along the right side until I was just below the passenger seat. I would only have one chance.

Muscles exploding, I lunged for the hat, snatched it from the seat, and took off across the fairway.

"Stop! Stop, you cur! I'll break your neck." Kurtz rammed his foot on the pedal of the cart, and it lurched forward.

I reached the cart path, slowed, and turned. Kurtz gripped the wheel, shoulders hunched, his eyebrows forced together in a vicious glare.

I let him get closer.

"I'll strangle you with my bare hands. Drop that cap, now."

And you're a buzzard's uncle, I thought, as I spun and ran along the rough, headed for the high ground with the view of the Santa Rosa mountains and the stand of palm trees.

Kurtz powered after me. Only one of his hands was on the wheel now, because he was fumbling for something in the dashboard compartment.

Jaw set, I swung through the palms and down the hill. He wouldn't dare use the gun during the daytime with players around, would he? I would have to be very careful. I could outrun a cart, but not a bullet.

I crossed the parallel fairway, threading through a foursome of men and their fancy carts, figuring Kurtz wasn't crazy enough to shoot in the direction of the humans or risk damaging their expensive rigs.

Kurtz followed curving around the players. One of the men waved at him but the gesture was not acknowledged.

Nearing the club house, I turned left and took the cart path back toward the eighteenth green. At the green, I abandoned the path and zigzagged among a cluster of sand bunkers. I was nearing my destination.

Kurtz chose to swing around the bunkers, which was what I expected him to do. I faked left and trotted up the trough-shaped fairway heading toward the tee boxes far in the distance. The best way for him to catch up with me from his current position was to swing around the high knoll that kept golfers from seeing the eighteenth green when making their approach shot.

Kurtz's cart disappeared behind the hill. This was my chance. I reversed direction and headed straight for the place he would come out from behind the hill on my right. Without breaking stride, I dropped the hat on the fairway. My timing had to be perfect.

In his anger, Kurtz was careless of the angle his cart had achieved as it came around the knoll. I jumped from behind a thick bush right into his path, barking like a foxhound after a vixen.

He was so startled, he yanked his wheel left. The cart tilted, throwing Kurtz right on the seat. The shifting of his weight sealed the fate of the maintenance cart. It rolled on its side, then its hood, as it slid down over the edge of the lake, flinging Kurtz head first into the murky waters. Aided by the steep lip, the cart executed a majestic final roll and came to rest on its tires, sinking slowly in the mud.

Kurtz struggled to stand, but the bottom was slimy. His feet slid out from under him, and he went down on his rump. I heard carts approaching behind me. One of the drivers was laughing. Across the lake, on the patio of the clubhouse, a crowd gathered. People pointed at Kurtz and gestured to newcomers, who ran out from the dining room to see what had happened.

Kurtz turned from the crowd and fixed a malevolent stare on me. Unnoticed by the golfers clustered near the wreck who were offering him a retriever pole to grasp, I trotted to the edge of the lake and dropped the foul Pinehurst cap I had retrieved on the surface of the water. We both watched the hat ride the

34

current toward the landscaped waterfall at the end of the lake where, after a pummeling among the rocks, it would disappear forever down the cavernous storm drain that ran under the property. After one last look at my soggy nemesis, I turned and loped toward the delivery gate and freedom.

# Chapter 11

 Smug as a roadrunner with a juicy grass-hopper in his beak, I trotted toward Buddy's gate head high. After my triumph over Kurtz, I had run all the way up the mountain to the broad mesa where the Joshua trees grow. With the stars so bright, I felt I could leap up and grab one as effortlessly as taking a Frisbee in flight. I tore along the sand, yipping and singing. A joy this immense had not been mine for many seasons. Exhausted at last, I had curled in the hollow of a high boulder and, dreaming of Jamie, my gentle handler, fell asleep to the melody of the coyotes.

This morning I would have the added pleasure of seeing my friends' faces, especially Buddy's, who had met the despicable Kurtz, when I told my story. Of course, Bud would also be thanking me for the cheese omelet surprise. It was going to be a very good day.

Javier saw me coming and met me at the Swindell's mailbox. "Mac, prepare yourself. More bad things have happened."

I rushed to the gate. Buddy faced away, his back to us.

"What's the matter, pal?" I tried to keep my voice steady."Did the omelet upset your stomach?"

Buddy remained the way he was.

"It's okay, big guy. We're your friends. To us, you always look good." Javier passed through the gate, walked around the towering poodle and sat where he could look him in the face. His amber eyes glistened under quivering brows.

Bud lowered his head toward Javier.

"Come on, Bud, Mac loves you."

The poodle straightened and turned slowly in my direction. I gasped before I could catch myself.

A deep, angry scar ran along Buddy's muzzle. Stitches held the red flesh together and black encrusted blood soiled the white fur on his jaw, neck, and upper chest.

"Who did this to you?" I was up off my haunches, every muscle taut, ready for a scrap. "I'll make him wish he'd never been weaned."

"She." Buddy sighed. "I'm afraid I've made a mess of things again."

"You've made a mess? Somebody's made a mess of you!"

"Mr. Swindell took me to a family that had another dog, a Doberman Pinscher. I thought it would be nice to have a new friend. I looked forward to the companionship, but Gerta didn't see it that way. You know how territorial we canines can be."

"Don't make excuses for her. Dobermans own their own attitude problems," I said. "That dame had issues."

"When she tripped to the fact that her human expected her to continue to be the outside guard dog and that I was to be the inside trophy dog, she just lost it. Laid in wait until I went out for a pee and lit into me. I've got bites everywhere, but my face is where she really connected."

"She was gonna turn their trophy into an ugly duckling," Javier said.

"Does it look that bad?"

"No, no. Forget I said that," Javier jumped in. "You'll be handsome as ever in no time."

I leaned on the gate. "So family number three dumped you, because their first dog had anger management problems."

"No, they returned me because I bled on their white living room rug. I got away from Gerta and ran in the house, looking for a little sympathy. Boy, I guess you can't get anything on a human's rug. I understand about the peeing now, but the blood wasn't my doing. I mean, it was my blood, but, well, you know what I mean."

"The important thing is that you're okay." I reached through the gate and touched his preposterous tail.

"That and you're back with us, man." Javier spotted a puncture on Buddy's paw and licked it. "Keep this up and you are going to be in the Guinness Book of World Records."

"Some title. Most rejected pooch."

"Nothing so dumb," I said. "How about Boomerang Pooch, the dog who always comes back, no matter what."

A little smile curled Buddy's swollen lip for the first time that morning.

# Chapter 12

"They've abandoned you!"

"No Mac, they're not gone for good."

"What's all that in the trash then?"

"Stuff they've discarded. I guess these are the things they don't want to take with them."

I thought that Buddy was perhaps one of those things, but I kept it to myself.

"Look, there are Brianna's training wheels, her hula hoop, and some old skates. Things a college girl doesn't need anymore."

"Are you sure they are coming back?"

"Positive. I can see how much furniture is left inside by putting my paws on the sill and looking in the window. LuLu's L-shaped sofa is right where it always was. Besides, they left water for me. See?"

"How much water? It is getting hot, now. And where's your food?"

"Mac, you are such a worry wart."

"Humans usually give me good reason to be worried, especially your humans."

"You're so good to me, Mac. I wish every dog had a guardian to watch over them as you watch over me."

"Wishes don't stick to your ribs. I'm going to McDonald's to get you something meaty for dinner." I trotted down the driveway, but stopped at the sidewalk, turned and winked. "I'll try to score some fries, too."

"My favorite!" Buddy's ridiculous tail spun in anticipation.

The fast food joint was packed. I looked through the window at the stacked lines of sweaty people. Summer was upon us. Overhead fans twirled above the crowd, creating a breeze that stirred the streamers taped to the ceiling.

The hot air burned my nostrils as I sniffed around the trash bins. The pickings were good. I had noticed summer after summer that spiking temperatures caused some humans to lose their appetites. I nosed a bag of half-eaten fries into a sack carrying the remains of a chicken sandwich, took the bag between my teeth, and made for the alley.

As I cut through the streets of the subdivision on my way back to Buddy's, I passed kids in bathing suits playing with hoses in several of the yards. It was all I could do not to stop, set Buddy's dinner aside, and run through the cool spray. I decided I would come back for a good shower as soon as I had delivered my prize.

Buddy must have been thinking along similar lines. When I arrived at the gate, he was coming up the steps out of the pool. When I dropped the bag and nudged it through the bars, he came over.

"How come you're not wet?" Puzzled, I stared at his dry coat.

"They drained the pool. There's still some water at the bottom though, so I was able to cool my feet off. If it gets real hot tomorrow, I'll roll in the puddle at the deep end."

Despite the heat, a chill fear griped my heart.

After saying goodnight to Buddy, I returned the way I had come, found two kids who were still playing, and cavorted with them until I was soaked to the skin. My dripping coat came in handy in the alley behind my favorite pizza place. A surly bum tried to corner me as I munched on a slice of pepperoni combo, so I indulged in a good shake. When I finished gyrating, he was wetter than I was.

With a full tummy and a cooled down coat, I trotted along Ramona Street toward Javier's neighborhood. It was still light when I turned on his street. I spotted the little guy and Dumb Derek sitting on the curb next to the fire hydrant.

"Boy, am I glad to see you, Mac." Derek's tongue dangled out of the left side of his mouth, the healthy pink center surrounded by a burnt orange edge.

Javier rubbed his back on the hydrant. "Derek is confused about the route home, and if I try to leave with him, Juanita will catch me."

Juanita was riding her bicycle in big circles on the Borrego's driveway.

"Happy to oblige, Derek. What brought you over this way in the first place?"

"He can't remember, Mac." Javier looked at me, his eyes going in figure eights.

A scream across the street attracted our attention. A large boy was squirting his younger siblings with a hose, holding his finger over the end to produce a powerful spray. His little sister squealed and jumped as the stream hit her on her bare midriff.

"I remember now! I'm tracking the dog that looks just like me!"

"Can't be many of those. Dogs with orange paws that glow in the dark are a rarity," I said.

"Wait until you see him. He could be my twin."

Derek leaped off the sidewalk and trotted across the road to a large puddle that had accumulated next to the curb where the boy was using the hose. He bent his heavy head and studied the surface of the water.

"Javier, he's seeing his reflection."

"What a dunce!"

43

Derek circled the water and found the right angle. "There he is! Hey, you, come out of there. I've been tailing you for blocks."

"Pathetic. I am so embarrassed for him." Javier draped a paw over his eyes.

"Those chemicals messed his brain cells up something fierce."

The boy with the hose noticed Derek and swung the nozzle in his direction. The spray blasted Derek and disturbed the surface of his puddle.

"Where'd he go?" Our friend spun around looking. "I've lost him again."

As I watched, a familiar sound caused me to rise and tense. The Hummer was near. I looked down Javier's street. The dark behemoth finished the turn and accelerated in our direction, spraying a passing cyclist with gravel. A growl escaped my throat.

"Steady, Mac. You've got to learn to resist these urges."

I could see the evil face at the wheel now. The man saw something that made him smile. He leaned forward and stepped on the gas.

I turned. Derek had found his reflection again, but he was in the traffic lane oblivious to the danger.

"Derek! Run!"

"I've got you now, twin." His face almost touching the puddle, Derek ignored me.

I shot forward. Willing my claws to deliver better traction, I flew across the street. The smell of the hated engine's heat assaulted my nostrils as I shot out between the parked cars.

I hit Derek in the hindquarters, sending him sprawling into the water and against the curb despite his bulk.

"MacKenzie!" Javier screamed.

I stared up at Derek's horrified eyes as the wave of pain surged up my legs. I could not move. My head lay in the water.

A quavering reflection captured my attention. It was the face of the hated one looking down, framed in an open door.

I shifted my head slightly and looked at the real driver. A grin of triumph spread across his ugly face. He slammed the door. The car started to move.

"Noooooo!" someone screamed, as the back tire of the Hummer rolled over my haunches.

Javier was by my side. "Mac, Mac, try not to move." He nudged his little body under my head like a pillow, keeping my cheek out of the water.

"Javier, listen. You have to help Buddy. He is in big trouble." A curtain of blackness closed over my eyes. "Get Derek to carry stuff for you."

"Mac, hang on."

I could feel his heart beating against my temple. It was hard to breathe. I tried to focus on Derek's rhythmic whimpers, but the sounds were fading.

"Help Buddy." My nose pressed hard against Javier's chest because I could no longer raise my head, his spunky scent all that remained of my world.

# Chapter 13

 I woke in the high desert. I could not imagine how I had gotten out of the city. It was so bright I could not keep my eyes open at first. I would have to find a way to shelter myself from the midday sun and locate some water, or this Border Collie was going to be toast.

As I squinted at the brilliant landscape, I saw a figure approaching in the distance. It was another dog, but what a dog! A powerful German Shepherd, he flew toward me, closing the vast space between us. I had heard about white shepherds but I had never seen one before. His fur was so healthy and groomed it glowed in the strong light, and his strides across the sand were as effortless as the glide of a red-tailed hawk.

I rose in preparation for the greeting ritual, hoping I had not given offense by encroaching on his personal territory.

The handsome dog approached and sat at a respectful distance. "Welcome, traveler. Welcome to Haven."

"Thanks. My name's MacKenzie. I'm from Yucca Dunes." I tried to get a look at my fur in my peripheral vision. I hoped I was presentable.

"Nice town."

"You know it? Good. I seem to have lost my bearings. Am I far from home?"

"You are in Paradise Valley."

This was not a valley I knew. "I hope you can show me how to get home from here, if it wouldn't be too much trouble."

"They call me Sonny."

"Nice to meet you, Sonny." I smiled, wondering if I could get him to pick up the pace a bit without being rude. I had to get back to Buddy. We circled and touched noses. A thrill of ecstatic joyousness traveled from my nose to the tip of my tail. His muzzle must have picked up static from running so fast.

I inhaled, sat back on my haunches and almost fell over backward, the sensation was so powerful. "Phew, I must be light-headed from my journey."

"It's the atmosphere here in Haven. That and your new appendages." Sonny ran his paw along my shoulders and pulled. "They're still a little damp. See if you can use your muscles to spread them out."

Panicked, I circled, like Derek chasing his tail. Something shifted on my left shoulder and drooped to the ground, pulling me off balance. "What's the matter with me? I can't stand up straight."

"Don't worry. Happens to all our new arrivals. You'll get used to them in no time. Here, let me help."

"*Don't.*" I almost said, "*Don't touch me.*" I realized how that would sound. "All I need is a drink of water. I'll be fine, and I can be on my way."

"You don't need water any more. You're welcome to drink it. But you don't need it."

"We're in a desert." Perhaps Sonny was as lost as I was and as much in need of life-saving water to get his head straight.

"We're in a desert because I thought a desert would look familiar to you. Give you comfort. If you had come from Maine, I would have arranged a different terrain."

"I don't follow." My suspicions were confirmed. Sonny was delirious.

"Haven is for every dog. It has to work for every dog no matter where you come from or the circumstances of your arrival."

"I'm sure it's a lovely place, but I can't stay. I have something to take care of. It's urgent."

"You'll find your priorities have changed."

"Hey, buster. Nobody messes with MacKenzie's missions, you got that?"

"Buddy will meet his own destiny."

I froze. "Who are you?"

"They call me the Good Shepherd."

"I see." I didn't see and I didn't care. I was going to have to start pushing back. "Well, would you be so good as to show me the way out?"

"Actually, you're not allowed out again, until you have learned to use those things on your back. We have a very efficient orientation program, if you'll just come this way." The white dog turned and trotted off.

I sat. He became a pinprick. I blinked. He sure could move. The pinprick started to get bigger. I guess he realized I wasn't behind him.

Sonny was almost to me when he halted, stood on his haunches and two enormous wings erupted from his shoulders. He began to wave them, and he rose.

A whirlwind of sand swirled up, blowing in my direction. I loped right to avoid it, but it was on me before I had gone two strides. The sand enveloped me, creating a dark cocoon. Out of the wind, Javier called my name, over Derek's wails. "MacKenzieeeeeeee." A pain tore at me. And I saw the hated face looking down.

The face and the sand vanished. I spun around looking for Javier, but I was back in the blinding white desert next to the white shepherd.

"I'm sorry I had to do that. Make you feel pain again. I assure you all that is over. I just needed you to remember."

"What?"

"Your accident."

"It was no accident." The gleam of the Hummer as it sped away filled my mind.

"I understand. But that's not the point. Is it?"

"The point is, I'm ..."

"Yes."

I jumped to my paws, closed the distance and shoved my muzzle in his face. "The point is I have to get back, go down, reverse direction, or whatever you want to call it. I have a friend to help. Let me go. Right now."

"No can do."

I lowered my head and started to pace the circle of attack around the shepherd. He was bigger than I was and muscular. I could not forget seeing him run like the wind, or unfurl his wings, but I would take him. I had to, for Buddy.

My white adversary studied me, the hint of a smile teasing his lip. He sighed and snorted on the ground, raising another cloud of sand.

Good move, I thought, spreading my paws for balance to take his first lunge.

The granules settled, and there stood Howie.

# Chapter 14

 While I was trying to comprehend the miraculous appearance of my long dead pal, Howie, Javier was up to his snout in problems. He told me his neck muscles almost gave out.

Javier had pushed against the window screen in the Borrego living room, nose pressed to the track until his skin was raw and his back was radiating pain in waves. Dejected, he sat on the sill. He realized he would have to come up with another approach.

Javier watched the boys toss their football in the adjacent yard. The blond boy threw the ball in a high arc. The boy with the spiky hair caught it and returned it as a low, rising bullet. The ball slammed the other kid in the abdomen, causing him to double over the projectile. The blond kid dropped the ball to the ground and sank beside it.

Javier stared at the pigskin, his eyebrows forced forward like antennae. He jumped to his feet, turned and shoved the window slide as far back as it would go, revealing the full expanse of screening. He hopped to the carpeting, ran to the far side of the room, whirled, and scraped his hind feet on the floor like a bull ready to charge.

"I can hit as hard as that ball, *chico*." He spat and went into action. Halfway across the living room, he went airborne. Executing a half roll, he hit the screen square in the middle with the full length of his body. The screen popped and fell on the shrubs lining the front of the Borrego house. Its momentum carried it over, and Javier was catapulted onto the lawn.

"Ahhhhh, *carumba*." He rubbed his shoulder with his jaw. "That hurt, but it hurt you more than me, *Señor* Screen."

Javier circled Derek, trying to herd him into the alley behind the Taco Bell. "We've got to pick up food, Derek, and carry it to Buddy."

"Okay, but why are we here?"

"Because this is where we find the food, remember?" Javier studied the Rottweiler's face for any sign of recognition that Derek recalled the strategy they had gone over and over.

The Mutt and Jeff team arrived at the dumpster at the Taco Bell. Trash spilled out of the giant container onto the pavement. Javier started rifling through the crumpled bags. After tunneling under a tall pile, he looked up. "Derek, stop eating! If you find something, set it aside for Buddy."

"Huh?"

Javier crawled out of the trash and stood in front of the chewing dog. "We are not here for us, we are here to get food for Buddy. Buddy will starve if we don't do this."

"Starving is bad. I know this." Derek nodded, staring into the middle distance.

"You know this stuff, Derek. Watch me." Javier ran to the pile, sniffed and yanked a bag from the pile, backing over to where Derek sat. "See, this is a burrito. For Buddy."

"For Buddy." Derek walked to the dumpster, rose on his hind legs and grabbed a sack. He brought it to Javier and dropped it at his feet.

Javier peered into the bag. "Tacos! Bravo!"

Fifteen minutes later, the two dogs stood at the busy Palm Tree Street intersection waiting for the light to change.

"This stuff smells awful good." Derek, who gripped the sack with the leftovers between his teeth, mumbled.

"Remember, *amigo*, that food is not for you. Besides, you ate six pounds of scraps before we left Taco Bell. You can't possibly be hungry." Javier paced to and fro at the edge of the crosswalk.

"There he is, Papa!" Juanita leaned across her mother's lap pointing as Mr. Borrego eased his truck to the curb.

"Oh, no. They'll take me home." Javier tried to hide himself behind Derek's rump.

"Come here, you little devil." Mr. Borrego stooped and swept Javier up in one broad, calloused hand.

"Derek, listen to me. Go directly to Buddy's house. You hear? Go now."

As the truck pulled away, the big dog set the bag on the curb. His fleshy forehead wrinkled in thought, Derek sank to the ground, panting.

Buddy sat on the bottom of the pool near the deep end. The growls from his stomach echoed off the steep walls. It had been three days since he had eaten the last of his dry food. There were about two bowls worth of water left in the pool. Now that there was so little of it, it was evaporating fast.

Javier had come with the terrible news. Mac was dead, killed by the same wicked man who had run down Howie. Buddy had felt something like this was bound to happen, the way Mac pursued the Hummer every chance she got. Yet in the end it had not been her doing. She had died a hero trying to rescue Derek.

Buddy got up and climbed the steps out of the empty pool. Night was here, and it would be cool enough to sit on the concrete by the gate.

Javier had promised to bring food. He said he was enlisting Derek so that the big dog could do the heavy lifting. Buddy knew Derek was not the brightest bulb in the streetlamp, but with Javier providing the brains for the operation, Buddy thought he had a reasonable chance of eating in the near future. He rested his shaggy head against the bars and willed the loyal Chihuahua to appear.

Derek pulled himself to his feet, picked up the bag and crossed the street. He reached the other side and rested the parcel on the sidewalk.

"I am supposed to go somewhere important. Can't remember where though." Derek looked down the street one way, then the other.

The Rottweiler looked down at the bag. "Seems I could get there faster if I just ate this stuff instead of having to carry it."

Derek's big muzzle disappeared into the bag.

# Chapter 15

"Your gray is gone, and your legs are straighter." I circled my old friend, admiring the shine of his golden coat.

"If you don't stop going around like that, I'll get dizzy." Howie's tongue dangled like a flag on a limo in a motorcade. "You leave arthritis behind when you come to Haven, so my elbows are back where they are supposed to be."

Looking at his sweet mug, I started to feel welcome. I shook my head to dispel the sentiment. "Howie, seeing you is the best. But I can't stay. Buddy is in trouble."

Howie's eyes strayed to the horizon. His big chest expanded as he drew in air. His exhale was long and steady. "Buddy will probably be joining us shortly. You must be patient. He will come."

"No. What is happening to him is wrong."

"On that we all can agree." The shepherd spoke in a low, firm tone.

"Howie, help me take these wings off." I swiveled my head, trying to see how the things were attached.

Howie's jowl wrinkled. "Gee, Mac, I don't think anybody has tried to take them off."

"Always a first time. Grab this and yank."

"That won't work." The shepherd was on his feet, frowning at me. "No one can take them off."

"Then find me the dunce who puts them on and have him do it." I was yelling in his face.

The shepherd sat back on his haunches as if I had punched him in the chest. "You are a disturbing presence, newcomer. You reject what is of great value. You do not consider the consequences to others."

Howie went to the white dog and rubbed against him. "It'll be okay, Sonny. She's just a little rough around the edges. The main thing is she has a heart of gold."

"The main thing is I don't want to be here because somebody needs me in Yucca Dunes."

"You are stubborn. There is much you don't know," the shepherd said.

"I don't have time to learn right now."

Now Howie was at my side, smoothing my hackles down into place. "Mac, give me a minute at least. If Buddy weren't in the mess he's in, you wouldn't be so hot to blow this joint? Am I right?"

"Well. It's just that he only has me."

"Okay. But what if we were able to, ah, send somebody to fix things? If you were assured that he would be safe?"

"Keep talking." I sat down to show my friend I was a reasonable dog, willing to listen. I had been rude, no question.

Howie returned to Sonny's side. He plunked his considerable bulk down in front of the shepherd and waited.

Sonny raised one eyebrow. "What she wants will disturb the balance. It cannot be done."

Howie said, "Great One, I understand what is at stake. I know I am not the smartest pup in the litter, but I have a suggestion. Would you do me the honor of hearing me out?"

# Chapter 16

Javier lurked behind a stack of newspapers on the far side of the Borrego garage. His chance to escape the house had come when *Mamacita* Borrego returned her mop to the rack on the garage wall. Now all he had to do was wait for *Señor* Borrego to come home from work and put the truck away.

This time he would carry the food himself. He couldn't manage much, so he would have to make multiple trips.

Javier heard the truck engine approach the double door. As the door began to rise, he scurried under the sedan so he would be nearer the opening and hidden from *Señor* Borrego's view. When *Señor* Borrego stepped on the accelerator easing the truck into the adjacent space, Javier sprinted for the driveway, praying *Señor* Borrego wouldn't look in his rearview mirror.

Javier made it to the Der Wienerschnitzel and scored an extra long all-beef wiener from the trash. Trotting with it between his teeth, he looked like a circus tightrope walker treading high above the center ring with his balance bar.

Exhausted, he reach Buddy's gate and set the drooping hotdog on the grass. "Buddy, I have food!"

He waited. There was no answer. I'll leave this and go to him. Once my strength returns, I'll drag it inside the yard.

Javier passed through the bars and along the cement walk to the backyard. "Buddy?"

He looked down into the swimming pool. His friend lay in the shadows in the deep end. "Buddy!" Javier circled to the stairs, hopped down them to the bottom of the pool and ran to Buddy's side.

"I have food for you, *amigo*. Wake up."

Buddy raised his head. It looked to Javier like the effort took all the poodle's strength. "You came. I knew you would not forget me."

Buddy's voice was weak and scratchy. Javier spun and made for the stairs. His friend needed the hotdog pronto.

As Javier approached the gate, he heard scuffling. He poked his head through the bars and gasped.

Two ravens were fighting for the wiener, bashing their wings at each other and tearing at the food.

"No, stop!" Javier charged, but the larger raven stood his ground. The bird was bigger than the Chihuahua.

As the little dog watched, the thing gulped down the meat.

# Chapter 17

"I don't believe in angels." I kept walking.

"So you told Buddy," Howie said.

"Hey, cut that out."

"Cut what out?"

"Reading my mind."

"So you think I'm a mind reader?"

"I think you are a pain." I scanned the horizon. There had to be some landmark that would suggest a way out of Paradise Valley. There was a cleft in the mountains, but the mountains looked very far away. If I hadn't known better, I'd have said they were receding. No matter, I had to find my way home on my own. Howie was being a bozo and wouldn't help.

"You realize the mountains will never get any closer." Howie had grown tired of walking and hovered over me gliding on the air currents. His wings, which were the same golden color as his coat, gleamed in the sunlight.

I stopped and rested my rump on the warm white sand. Howie banked, landed, and settled next to me.

"Looks like your shepherd friend is coming back." I indicated a pinprick on the horizon.

Howie stood and shivered, his feathers dancing in the breeze. "Oh, please, let him bring good news."

Sonny materialized before us in a vortex of spinning sand crystals. "I see you persist in your attempt to leave Haven," he said as he smoothed his fur.

Howie circled the white dog. "Tell us, Sonny. What has been decided?"

Sonny folded his wings. "Howie, your proposal has been accepted."

Howie rolled in delight, his feet pointing skyward, his feathery ears making angels in the sand. "Oh, mercy, mercy."

Sonny turned to me. "There are, however, two conditions."

"Having to do with me?" I knew there would be some kind of hitch. I could not keep my eyes from narrowing into suspicious slits.

"First, you have to acknowledge your situation. And second, you have to stop trying to leave and accept your place here in our community. Then, and only then, will we deal with Buddy's dilemma."

"So, it's all on me is it?" I turned my back on them and resumed my march to the mountains.

"How do your legs feel?" Sonny asked.

"Getting kind of personal, aren't ya?"

"Anything feel broken?"

"What the ..."

The shepherd was above me, circling. He picked up speed, and the sky beyond him blurred into a satin halo. I realized I was getting dizzy, but I could not stop spinning to keep Sonny in view. The world around me melted and a fuzzy image formed in its place. I saw myself lying on a street. At my head was a puddle of water. Under my paws was a pool of blood. My limbs rested at an odd angle.

The fuzzy picture was accompanied by distorted sounds. Javier was speaking to me and Derek hovered on the edge of the shifting image, crying. The sounds of the two dogs blended into a mournful echo that rose and fell along with my breathing. Then the image started to recede like the mountains I was trying to reach. It fell away from me down a long tunnel until it was nothing more than a speck. Finally, it danced off in a crazy spin like the ghost images I saw on the insides of my eyelids when I pressed them together too hard.

I squeezed my eyes shut in an involuntary reaction. When I opened them, Sonny was standing back where he had been before he went airborne.

"How do your legs feel?"

Hadn't he already asked me that? "They feel fine if it's any of your business."

He didn't respond.

I sauntered off trying not to look at my legs. I didn't want to give Sonny the satisfaction. A breeze teased the sand on the desert floor and rippled my fur. A whisper of sound caused me to turn and concentrate. It sounded like Derek howling.

Why had Derek been howling? And Javier? Why was his little face so twisted with anguish?

# Chapter 18

Javier flung bags left and right, frantic to find a discarded burger or fish fillet. Panic tore at his heart. He moved to the next dumpster. Lying near the rusted wheel was a half filled bag of curly fries. Javier bunched the top of the bag in his jowls and took off.

"Say it, Mac," Howie pleaded. "Out loud."

They were double teaming me.

"Denial is very common," Sonny said."You need to move to the next level."

"Acceptance, Mac." Howie nuzzled me. "You can do this."

I shoved him away. "Doesn't it ever get dark here?"

"Night? No problem." Sonny lifted his face skyward and howled a rich rising wail. The sky blackened to velvet. "Moon? Milky Way?" he asked.

I refused to answer.

Sonny barked two short barks. We were bathed in moonlight and the frothy constellation floated overhead like a feather in a spring breeze.

Howie looked at me and frowned. "Maybe he needs a different kind of proof."

"Maybe so." Sonny rose and padded to a location a dozen feet away. He studied the twinkling sand for a moment, turned and began to dig with his back feet, sending curtains of sand in the air.

The flying particles looked like ice shavings or fire flies. They sparkled in the moonlight, an army of fairies.

"That should do it." Sonny stopped digging, sat and admired his work.

As they settled, the crystals changed the surface of the desert floor. We were looking at a square dark rectangle.

"It's a swimming pool!" Howie rushed forward and peered over the edge. I followed.

Although the moon's rays could not reach the bottom, a soft glow appeared on the floor of the pool, down at the deep end.

Javier dragged the bag down the steps of the pool. He could not carry the bag down because it was so big. He could not see his feet. He jumped down a step and pulled the sack over after him.

He reached the bottom and tried to lift the bag, but he was too exhausted. He dragged it along, backing toward Buddy.

When his back paw touched one of the poodle's big fluffy feet, he knew he had reached his goal. "Buddy, I have fries."

Javier turned and studied the prone dog. Nothing moved. He could not see Buddy's eyes because the poodle lay in the shadows.

"Buddy, wake! Please wake up" Javier rushed to the big dog and nuzzled his soft topknot. "I've brought your favorite."

The head moved a fraction, but did not lift up.

"*Amigo*, please. Here, I will feed you." The little dog dragged the bag over, pulled a fry out and placed it next to Buddy's lips. "Please try."

"I'm sorry. I can't." Buddy's voice was a whisper.

"No! I won't let you die." Javier upended the bag and shoved the fries as close to Buddy's mouth as he could.

"Come sit by my head, dear Javier. Stay with me, 'til it's over."

Weeping, head drooping, the Chihuahua staggered to the poodle and collapsed into a ball, resting his head on the bigger dog's cheek.

I prowled the edge of the pool watching the scene unfold. "We have to stop this. There's no time."

Sonny and Howie sat together on a dune, their backs to the full moon. I left the pool edge and trotted to a position in front of the two dogs, snorting in my frustration.

They remained silent. The only sound was the lonely moan of the desert wind.

I looked over my shoulder at the dimming image of Buddy and Javier and back at Howie and Sonny. "I'm ..."

Howie smiled and nodded, encouraging me.

"I died in an accident. I was run over by the evil one. Same as you, Howie." My lip edged up revealing my fangs as I remembered him laughing at me lying in my own blood. "I'm dead. There, I said it."

"And the other condition?" Sonny prompted.

"Yes. I will stay."

I ran back to the pool edge. The image had vanished. I whirled and returned to the dune. Sonny was gone.

# Chapter 19

Dawn came to Yucca Dunes, but it was a puny, tentative light. The straw-colored rays tiptoed across the floor of the Swindell pool until they reached Javier's diminutive eyelids. Javier's eyes opened. Remembering, he rested his head once more on the unruly pompadour atop the poodle's head.

"I did not leave you, *amigo*," he sighed.

Buddy's body was cold now. He was heavy and still and his smell had changed. Javier rubbed his head along the curly fur. At least Buddy's wooly ringlets were the same.

Javier placed a kiss on the silent muzzle. "I will never forget you, my friend." He walked a few paces toward the stairs, but turned back. "And I will never forget the evil one who set this tragedy in motion. No, never."

From his perch on the Swindell's roof, Sonny watched the Chihuahua make his mournful way up the stairs, around the house, and out the gate. When the coast was clear, he unfurled his wings and glided to the head of the steps.

Sonny barked. Once. Twice. Three times.

Somebody has come to call, Buddy thought. I had better go and greet him. It is not a song I recognize.

Buddy headed for the steps. Sitting at the top was a giant of a German Shepherd, white as the waves in White Water Canyon.

"You must be a powerful jumper to get over my wall, but you are welcome." Buddy stepped out of the pool and sat on the tile apron.

"Thank you, Buddy."

"You know my name!"

"I know the name of every dog. It is my gift." The shepherd gestured toward the block wall that surrounded the yard. "As to your wall, I can't let a little obstacle like that get in the way of my mission."

"A mission? How exciting. I never get to do anything exciting."

"If you wished for something exciting, what would it be?"

"I would wish to live with a certain lady."

"What's so special about this lady?"

"Oh, she is the queen of special. She looks into your eyes. She touches you. Here." Buddy indicated the special place, his eyes moistening.

"Ah, there. That is special," the shepherd said. Then he shook himself as if shaking off a memory. "I am going to make your wish come true."

Buddy's mouth opened but nothing came out. He looked like a lawn ornament with fur.

"How long have you been living in this awful place?"

"Three years." Buddy hung his head.

"Buddy, because you have been so mistreated, you are going to get your wish. However, you will get to live with the wonderful lady for exactly six years, twice the amount of time, you have been abused." The shepherd turned Buddy so that he was facing the pool.

Buddy saw himself lying still, in the deep end. He gulped and sat down hard.

"You see, I can only postpone what fate has decreed. If I do more, I will disturb the balance."

Buddy descended the steps and stood over his remains. He circled his body, walked slowly back to the bottom of the steps and looked up at the shepherd.

"I see how it is. Six years with the lady is more happiness than I can even imagine. I will savor every moment. And when my time is up, I will go as we have agreed."

"Good, it's settled."

"But how will you find her? I don't even know her name."
"Leave everything to the Good Shepherd."

Just before lunch time, Yucca Dunes experienced one of those rare, violent rain storms that bring the desert flowers into bloom, carry away a few vehicles left parked in low places, and take out the electricity in a neighborhood or two.

"Hey, fellow, what are you doing down there?" The power company lineman shinnied down the pole behind Buddy's back-yard. The dog was sitting in a foot of water at the bottom of a swimming pool, and he looked like he did not have the strength to drag himself up the steps.

The lineman stepped off the pole onto the wall that bounded the property. "Looks like nobody's home," he said as he studied the back of the shuttered house. The man lowered himself into the yard, descended into the pool and got an arm under the dog's torso. "Come on, boy. Let's get you out of here."

He set the dog down under the eave that protected the kitchen door. "When was the last time you ate, big guy?" The man scanned the area for a bowl.

Buddy looked up at the man, but the effort made him stagger.

"You wait. I've got just the thing." The man disappeared over the wall. Buddy heard a vehicle door open and close, and the man returned with a lunch pail.

"My wife makes me these baloney sandwiches. I hate balo-ney. Here, you take 'em." He watched the dog gulp down the first of the two sandwiches, even eating the lettuce. "With this rain, I want something hot today anyway. I'll stop at McDonald's, but before I do, I'm going to call Animal Control about you."

# Chapter 20

The following morning two cars arrived at Buddy's place: the Swindells returning from their trip, and, an hour later, an official van with a big round seal emblazoned on the door.

Lulu burst through the kitchen door carrying a bowl of dog food. She put the bowl in front of Buddy. "Hurry, Buddy, eat this."

The door opened again and Warren emerged, followed by two people in khaki uniforms. The man who held a clipboard continued to talk with Warren, while the woman advanced on Buddy. She held her palm out for him to smell. "Hey, big boy, let me examine you."

The woman felt Buddy's ribcage, checked his ears, pulled his eyelids back so she could inspect his pupils and lifted his lips to study his gums. "Write the citation, Hal. This dog is rail thin and dehydrated."

Warren Swindell's face turned red as he accepted the citation from the officer. The man returned his pen to his starched shirt pocket. "We will return in a week to check on the dog. His condition and his circumstances need to show improvement, or we will be citing you again, Mr. Swindell, and removing the dog for his own protection."

His stomach comfortably full, Buddy snoozed the afternoon away. At five o'clock, he was awakened by a commotion in the garage. He circled the house to the side gate to see what he could. Lulu had backed the station wagon up to the garage door, and Warren had dragged the big carrier out of the garage. He opened the rear hatch, slid the carrier into the wagon, and unfastened the cage door.

Lulu opened the gate to the yard and grabbed Buddy's collar. "Come on, we've found another place for you to live." She pulled Buddy to the wagon and patted the spot in front of the carrier's gaping door.

Because he was still weak, it took Buddy two tries to get in. I am to be given away to another of Mr. Swindell's acquaintances who has money, Buddy reasoned. Dejected he settled into the carrier, and Lulu slammed the hatch.

As Swindell sped down the street, Buddy scanned the sidewalk for one last sighting of Javier or Derek. "I will never see my friends again, and my dream of living with the wonderful lady was just that. Only a dream."

That angel of a shepherd must have been a product of his imagination, brought about by thirst and starvation, he concluded. Buddy curled himself into a ball on the floor of the carrier and pulled a huge ear over his eyes.

Buddy must have fallen asleep during the long ride. He bolted upright when startled by the slam of the driver's door. The station wagon was parked on a wide circular driveway edged in flowers. Buddy could make out the lavender blossoms of a bush on one side of the car, but could not see where Mr. Swindell went because of the positioning of his carrier.

He dozed off again, his muzzle resting on his paws, so he was jolted awake a second time when Mr. Swindell opened the hatch.

"Okay, Bud, this is it. This is your new home." Swindell got hold of Buddy's collar and started dragging him from the box. Although Buddy's home with the Swindells was no picnic, it was all he had known, so he dug his feet in.

"Stupid dog. Stop your struggling." Swindell put his hands under Buddy's armpits and yanked.

Once Buddy was on the driveway, Swindell guided him to a gate in the wall surrounding the house, and shoved him through. "They've got a bigger yard. Better for your size."

The gate was solid unlike Buddy's old gate, so he could not see Swindell drive off, only hear him start the engine.

"He could have at least said goodbye." Buddy turned and, hanging his head, treaded slowly toward the rear of the house. The yard was huge and landscaped. There were palm trees, jacarandas and palo verde trees, bushes of every description and, the most surprising thing of all, grass. Buddy gave a little moan of pleasure as he set his paws down on the luxuriant, cool surface.

Ahead of him, shimmering in the growing dark, was a large pool with a burbling waterfall. Pool reflections danced on the ceiling of a porch brimming with furniture that ran the length of the house.

Buddy walked to the edge of the pool, rimmed in cheery tiles. A turquoise float bobbed on the surface.

"Welcome to my home." A voice came from the shadows of the porch.

Buddy's head snapped up and his nostrils wrinkled with the effort of catching the other's scent. Oh no, he thought, they already have a dog. It will be like the last time with Gerta.

The scar on his nose itched as he remembered her assault. A shadow moved from the shelter of the porch toward the pool.

"I am Skootch, master of this domain. You must be Buddy. They have been speaking of you inside."

Buddy studied the other dog. Skootch, a mature German Shorthaired Pointer, was thickening around the middle and beginning to bow a little at the elbows. A dusting of gray hairs softened the black circle of fur around his left eye and ear. Surely, a dog like this won't have Gerta's temperament, he hoped.

Skootch came closer, sniffing. "Clear up one thing. You are just visiting aren't you?"

Buddy's hopes, which had been rising with the realization that Skootch was no attack dog, fell with the knowledge that the older dog did not want a companion. "I'm afraid I'm meant to be permanent. My people don't want me anymore."

"That's rough." Skootch frowned, walked to the far end of the pool and stretched out on the pool deck, his back to Buddy.

I'm being rejected and I haven't even met the humans yet. What, Buddy wondered, can I say to make him like me?

Buddy approached the pointer, but stopped at a respectful distance. "Your home is very beautiful. I too lived alone, but my yard was nothing to compare to this."

"It is peaceful. There are many birds, roof rats, and the occasional rabbit."

"If you let me stay, I will respect your status. Maybe I can be helpful in some way."

"There is a lot to be responsible for. And I am not getting any younger. Perhaps you could be of use." Skootch rolled to his other shoulder so he could get a better look at the younger dog. "Can you bark with authority?"

"Oh yes, I can really make a statement. Would you like to hear a little something?"

"Well, we don't want to raise the whole neighborhood. Just give me a 'get lost you mangy cat' bark."

"Sure thing." Buddy cleared his throat, praying his recent experiences had not deprived him of his song. He barked. It wasn't his best. "Let me try that again. I've been through kind of a rough patch."

Skootch's ears perked at the sound of a sliding door being opened.

"I see you two have met." A human figure approached them. The face was in shadow, but the human's hair was backlit by the security lamp. It was a silver halo.

Buddy's heart slammed into his chest, and his eyes blinked. It's her! The Good Shepherd kept his promise. I am to be hers!

The wonderful lady handed Skootch a treat first, a large milk bone. The dog placed it between his paws and gnawed, his eyes closed in pleasure.

Buddy waited. She came over and presented him a bone. "Welcome, Buddy. I am very glad Mr. Swindell finally consented to bring you here."

Buddy took the bone, but it hung out the side of his mouth. He could not take his eyes off her face. She was touching him, rubbing the special place, and Buddy thought for the first time that he could live on love.

# Chapter 21

Derek circled back from his station by the side garden where he had been guarding the pile of cat litter and sat in front of Javier. "Why can't we find Buddy?"

Javier rested in the shadow of an olean-der bush. "We've been over this and over this, Derek. Buddy is dead. There's no point in going over to his house, because he is not there."

Derek nodded. "Okay, so where is he then?"

Javier sighed and got to his feet. This was one of those days when Derek was awake, but his brain cells continued to slumber. Javier cursed the chemicals that had turned his friend into a mental midget. "You stay here, pal, and keep an eye on that kitty poop. I've got something I have to do."

Javier planned to search the northwest corner of town for the Hummer that day. He would work from the edge of the airport back toward his own street. Since it was daytime, he would focus on places of business and restaurants. He could leave the residential streets for the late afternoon.

Searching for the Hummer was very hard work for a guy with such short legs, but Javier was determined to avenge Buddy, Howie, and me. Javier was not sure what he would do to the evil Hummer owner when he finally located him. Somehow, peeing on his tires was not going to do the trick, but Javier reasoned that he could figure out his approach later. First, he had to find the hated vehicle.

Javier walked the length of Airport Avenue and returned to his own neighborhood along Commercial Street. Exhausted, he stopped in the parking lot of the 7-Eleven and rested in the shade of the dumpster.

The rev of an engine drew his attention to the street. "It's the Hummer!" Javier was on his feet.

The huge vehicle pulled in front of the 7-Eleven. Half of the thing spilled over into the blue disabled space. The evil one jumped from the cab and entered the store.

Javier studied the Hummer. He examined the underside to see if there was a pocket or ledge where he could ride safely. Emerging from under the vehicle, he surveyed the back trying to find a place he could hang on. Nothing looked safe. Javier knew he would fall and be crushed by the Hummer's wheels or another car. His only recourse was to follow the man as fast as he could and try to keep the Hummer in sight. Traffic was heavy, so he had a chance. Javier sniffed the tires and the path the man had taken into the store, storing each molecule of scent so that he would recognize the smell anywhere he found it.

The man exited the store with a brown bag. He threw the bag on the seat, climbed into the Hummer and started the engine.

Javier pawed the ground and filled his lungs with air for the chase. The Hummer pulled out in traffic, taking its place in a line of slowly advancing cars.

Javier kept pace with the Hummer for four blocks. At the next light, the big car made a right turn on a residential avenue. "*Carumba*, these side streets don't have much traffic." Javier started trotting as the Hummer accelerated.

He almost caught the man at the stop sign, but the Hummer did not stop completely at the intersection and swerved around the corner heading south.

I'm going to lose him, Javier thought. He ran to the middle of the street so that he would be able to see which way the Hummer turned at the next corner.

The Hummer did not turn, but gunned across the four-way stop. A green sedan screeched to a halt as the big car muscled past. As the Hummer accelerated away, Javier stopped trotting and collapsed on the macadam.

I will just have to settle for following the scent, he thought, as he tried to get control of his panting.

In the distance, the Hummer turned right and vanished. "Hey, that's my street!" Javier took off trotting after the Hummer.

Javier made it halfway down the next block when he heard screams. He zigzagged between the parked cars and made a diagonal across the two remaining lawns to the corner. Careening around a pair of parked motorcycles, he pounded along the edge of the line of parked cars.

Near the end of the street, a knot of people took up both lanes of traffic. A siren pierced the air. "That's my house. *Mamacita!*"

*Señora* Borrego stood in her front yard supported by two neighbors, her face the color of a bed sheet.

"Oh, the feet, the feet." Javier fought off his terror and dove into the crowd, weaving in and out of the shuffling legs. When he gained the center of the mob, somebody kicked him. He fell against a heap of twisted metal, scratching his shoulder on a jagged edge.

"Ouch, watch your step, *Señor.*" Javier sniffed the metal object detecting a familiar smell. When his nose connected, his eyes made sense of the object.

"This is Juanita's bike!" Javier searched the milling legs for the little girl. "Juanita?"

Javier darted out of the crowd following his nose. He saw a policeman holding Papa Borrego by the shoulders, trying to talk to him, but *Señor* Borrego was looking over the officer's shoulder at his child's motionless body. Javier hurried to Juanita and buried his nose in her hair. "Juanita, it's me, your Javier."

Javier guarded the little girl on the stretcher. He had been able to jump up on the mattress, because the stretcher was on the ground. The smell of the Hummer was strong on her, and she still had not opened her eyes. Her lids fluttered though, and she moaned softly.

"Sorry, little fella." The ambulance driver lifted Javier to the ground and raised the stretcher into the travel position. He and another man rolled Juanita toward the ambulance.

Javier turned to find Papa Borrego. Another policeman had joined the first and a trio of neighbors were all talking to them at once. Their faces were red and their voices were angry. Papa Borrego did not look as if he were listening, and his fists, which he held stiffly against his slacks, clenched and unclenched to a silent rhythm.

Javier trotted to the intersection beyond the accident scene, chest tight and upper lip curved in a nasty snarl. I will find him, Javier promised himself. I will track him to the ends of the earth. He will not get away with this.

The Chihuahua zigzagged across the macadam, his nose an inch from the pavement. He stopped over a tire mark that swerved left down the parallel street. "You are toast, *diablo*." Javier tore along the tire impression like a wind-up race car on a toy speedway.

Leaving his own neighborhood, crossing Commercial Street and passing through another subdivision, Javier followed the scent into a tract of Santa Fe style houses. Two blocks into the subdivision, the smell turned up a driveway and disappeared under a double garage door.

Javier inhaled deeply from the crack between the door and the cement. The Hummer is in the garage! I can even smell a little of Juanita's bike.

He trotted into the flowerbed near the entrance to the home and positioned himself under a rosemary bush. From his position, he could see into the living room, but no one was there. I have to find help, Javier thought. I have to bring someone to this house and convince them the evil one is inside, but who can I bring? Papa Borrego will be with Juanita wherever they have taken her.

A grinding sound to his left made Javier almost jump out of his collar. He sneaked back to the edge of the driveway and peaked around the corner. The sound was from the garage door rising. The evil one exited the garage carrying a hose. He strolled to a spigot on the other side of the door and twisted the hose onto the connector.

"He is going to wash the car! I must not let this happen." Without thinking, Javier leaped from his hiding place and barked at the man.

Startled, the evil one looked up, but he quickly regained his composure and sneered at the Chihuahua. He aimed the spray gun at Javier and spun the water valve. "Wanna play, shorty?"

The force of the spray knocked Javier over, and he rolled down the driveway. He tried to stand, but the evil one kept the powerful stream of water on him. He rolled to the ditch at the edge of the street.

Laughing, the man tossed the hose aside and headed for him. Sputtering and squinting, Javier struggled to his paws, just as the evil one reached his big hairy hands for him. As the beefy fingers closed around him, Javier shot forward. The dog's soaked fur was an asset, and he popped from the man's grasp like a greased pig in carnival contest.

He ran up the street to the sound of the evil one's laughter. "I must find someone and fast."

Javier headed for Commercial Street. As he approached the Chevron station, his heart leaped. A patrol car was parked next to a police motorcycle. A man in a cap leaned on the patrol car, listening to a man in a helmet and sunglasses.

Javier came to a halt in front of the men and began to yip. The men turned and the helmeted one took off his sunglasses and spoke. "Hey, little fella, you're kinda small to be out on a busy street."

"See if he's got a tag, Fred."

The man with the sunglasses started toward him. Javier's eyes dropped to the boots he was wearing. The dog's body shivered from his nose to his tail, and his teeth began to chatter. "I can't do this." Javier shot away and hid behind the air and water kiosk.

He tried to get control of the shaking. "Okay, *amigo*, they mean you no harm, they just have very big feet." He peeked around the kiosk. The men had forgotten him and were back talking to each other.

"I must get their attention." Javier took a deep breath. "I've got to beat this thing." He swung out from behind the kiosk and trotted over to the officers.

"Look, the Chihuahua's back."

"Let me try this time." The man with the cap came toward him. "Here, boy."

Javier eyes drifted down the man's trousers to his shoes. The shoes were big and thick soled. Javier began to tremble. He must have an EEEEE foot, he thought, wider than my chest. Javier backed away.

"I'm not gonna hurt you." The man settled on his haunches and reached out, palms up and open.

Javier made himself stop backing up. "He can't step on you, dummy, if he is squatting. Get to business!" He approached the man, yipping as he went.

The man patted his head. Javier danced and ran in a circle, out to the intersection and back to the officer.

"Cute dog." The man with the boots came forward. Javier gritted his teeth, but kept circling.

"I think he wants us to follow him." The crouching man stood.

"Don't be silly, he's just playing."

"No, watch." The officer pointed.

"They're getting it!" Javier widened his circle. When he reached the apogee he stopped, and ran a few yards down the street he wanted them to take.

"He wants us to go down Montoya." The man dug in his trouser pocket for his keys. "I remember this dog. He was at the accident scene."

Javier returned to his position in front of the men and yipped, jumping up and down in place.

"You pace him on the cycle, and I'll follow." The man headed for the cruiser.

Javier cringed when the man swung his boot over the motorcycle. He jumped when the man turned the engine over. The thing sounded too much like the Hummer, but the dog gathered himself and trotted off down Montoya.

The man kept the cycle a respectful distance behind the little dog. Javier looked over his shoulder when he changed streets to make sure the man followed.

When he turned onto the evil one's street, he could see the back end of the Hummer, because it jutted out beyond the line of parked cars. The ebony rear of the Hummer gleamed in the late afternoon sun.

"He's washed the thing clean! How will I convince them this is the one?"

The patrol car pulled up as the other officer dismounted from the motorcycle. The evil one stopped hosing the hood of the vehicle and studied the officers. Across the street, a man who had been using a leaf blower turned it off, and signaled to his wife to stop weeding.

"This your Hummer?" the officer from the cruiser asked.

The man nodded and tossed his hose to the ground.

"A black Hummer was in a hit and run earlier today."

"That so." The man walked to the edge of his property right in front of the two officers and crossed his arms over his burly chest.

"Hit a little girl on a bike. She's going to make it, but she's banged up pretty bad."

"Don't know a thing about it."

Javier surveyed the vehicle, desperate to find evidence of the accident. As the men talked, he stole along the side of the huge auto to the right front tire. The Hummer was so tall, it was hard to imagine there would be any marks on the chassis. Javier examined the mammoth hubcap. Nothing jumped out but his own distorted reflection.

Javier walked to the front of the Hummer and slumped to the driveway. If there had been marks on the chrome, the evil one had had the time to buff them away. The nasty man was going to get away with it all. Get away with hurting little Juanita. Get away with killing Mac and Howie. Javier had tried, but he had failed.

He sighed and dragged himself off the pavement. As he passed the Hummer on his way to the street, he glanced at the massive tire. The thing winked at him.

Javier froze, thrust his head forward, his brows hunched like hedgerows. Embedded in the treads of the tire were dozens of shards of pink glass. Higher up on the tire, almost out of sight, a handful of streamers were caught, the party-colored streamers from the handlebars of Juanita's bike.

Javier barked. He barked, yipped, and yapped, bouncing in front of the forward tire.

"What the ..." The motorcycle cop was back astride his cycle, but he dismounted and put it back on its kickstand. The other officer started toward the Chihuahua.

"Stay off my property," the evil one snapped.

Javier ran toward the officers and back toward the tire.

"Hey, get away from there." The man rounded the back of the Hummer and made for Javier, his boots slapping the pavement so hard Javier could feel the vibrations.

The man's shadow swept over him. Javier's mouth gaped and he couldn't move.

Leaning forward, the man bent, grunted and snared a finger under Javier's collar. Javier felt his front feet lift off the ground.

He pulled his neck in like a turtle and twisted. His head popped out of the collar, leaving it dangling empty from the man's finger. He scampered to the tire, jumped up, and took one of the streamers in his teeth. In two yanks, he freed it. Jumping down, he sprinted under the Hummer and made for the officers.

The squad car door was ajar. Javier gathered himself, jumped, and landed on the policeman's lap and hopped to the passenger seat. He spit the streamer out on the leather.

The officer stared at the streamer, his eyes blinking. He frowned. "Hold on, boy." Without closing the door, he let the cruiser drift forward until it blocked the Hummer's exit from the driveway. When the car came to rest, he leaned forward and motioned to the other officer. "Fred, get a load of this."

A small crowd had gathered in front of the squad car. The man and his wife from across the street, a florist who had been making a delivery at the house next door, a mailman, a skate boarder and other bystanders.

"He's the hit and run man," somebody yelled. The Hummer man spun, ran up his walk and jerked at his front door. The door was locked. He ran back down the walk and around to the open garage door. He disappeared into the shadows of the garage. The slam of a door could be heard from the back of the garage, as the double door lowered into the closed position.

"He's got walls all around. He's too fat to get out the back," a woman said.

"We won't take any chances." The officer gunned his motorcycle.

"Coward," the florist yelled, "come out and face the music."

The other officer was speaking into a box on a curly-cue rope, and the box squeaked back at him. Javier heard sirens from two directions. The Chihuahua returned to the Hummer's front tire and stationed himself beside his find.

# Chapter 22

Buddy rode in the backseat of the station wagon, head out the window, ears flapping in the wind. Skootch was at the other window, his paw braced on the arm rest. The special lady, Deedee, and her daughter Maxine were taking the two dogs for a ride to Cousin Eliza's house. Maxine and Eliza were the women who had accompanied Deedee when Buddy first met his beloved lady. Maxine lived with Deedee in the big house with the heavenly yard. Eliza had been looking for a place of her own. It was Eliza who had bought the Swindell's house. This would be Buddy's first visit to his old digs since Eliza had acquired the home. Something told him that with Eliza's sunny personality and preference for colorful outfits, the old place was not going to be the same.

Deedee pulled into the driveway. Eliza waited at the gate to the backyard. When Deedee let Skootch and Buddy out of the wagon, Eliza swung the gate open. "Come on Skootch," Buddy said, "I'll show you where I used to hang out."

The two dogs passed through the gate and into the backyard. "Wow, she's performed a miracle." Buddy looked at the expanse of emerald grass, the sage bush, and the row of hibiscus shrubs. In the center of the lawn, a young palo verde tree stood, its base protected by a circle of wire mesh. Against the back wall, a row of rose bushes, in every imaginable color grew, tethered by little stakes.

"Where did all the cement go? Skootch, you can't imagine what it was like." Buddy sat near the back door, shaded by a large striped awning. "It so cool now. Before, you could fry an egg on this spot."

"Looks pretty inviting now." Skootch sauntered over and collapsed in the shade.

"You boys want to see the inside?" Eliza held open the door to the kitchen.

"Whoa, I was never allowed in the house." Buddy stepped onto the polished pavers of the remodeled kitchen.

"Remember what I taught you," Skootch said.

"I won't even think about lifting my leg." He and Skootch toured the entire house, admiring the thick carpets, rich draperies, and, in the cozy study, greeting Eliza's Manx cat, Betty Anne.

The dogs returned to the yard for a treat and fresh water. "What happened to that cat's tail?" Buddy asked.

"According to her, she's never had one. Says it makes her more mysterious," Skootch said. "She's gotta be lying. I figure she ran into a pooch with an attitude problem, lost her appendage, and is too embarrassed to admit it. You know how cats are."

"I haven't known many cats, but I've met a dog or two with a bad temper." Buddy remembered Gerta and wondered if she had gotten any help with her issues.

Buddy cocked an ear. He thought he detected the tap-tap of tiny claws on the familiar pavement. "Follow me, please." He raced around the house to the side gate.

Across the street on the sidewalk, a gaggle of dogs paraded. There were two Dachshunds, a Collie, an English Bulldog, a Bichon Frise, two young Labrador Retrievers, and a Schnauzer. In the lead was a Chihuahua wearing a red, white, and green collar flanked by a Rottweiler with orange feet.

"Javier. Oh, it's Javier. Javier!" Buddy jumped up on the gate.

Javier stared, his mouth agape. The other dogs milled around him, studying the stranger.

Derek bounded across the street. "Buddy, you were here all the time. I told him you were here."

Javier shook his head hard and rubbed his eyes. "*Amigo*?"

"It's me, pal." Buddy danced on his fuzzy legs. "The tall guy."

Javier shot across the street and through the bars. He wove in and out of Buddy's legs rubbing his head. The big dog put his head down and draped his ears around the Chihuahua. Tears ran down his snout onto the little dog.

"I thought you were dead. You were dead. It's a miracle," Javier said.

"It is a miracle all around. I am with the lady. Can you believe it? And look at this place. Talk about your miracles."

After being introduced to Skootch and introducing his friends, Javier toured the yard along with Dora Dachshund, who was slim enough to make it through the bars.

"That's some piece you're wearing," Buddy said, admiring the gold medallion dangling from his friend's collar. "You always were a dapper dresser."

"That's his award," Dora said. "Don't be modest, Javier, tell them."

Javier pursed his lips and rolled his eyes.

"Come on, Javier, tell us." Buddy came around to his side of the pool and stretched out in front of the little dog.

"Okay, okay. I found him, Buddy. The evil one. I found him and brought him to justice."

"They gave him a medal. The mayor said he was a hero. He is the most famous dog in the valley," Dora said.

"Dora heads my fan club." The Chihuahua nodded his head toward the gate. "These guys are my, ah, entourage."

"I always knew you had it in you, Javier. Mac and Howie would be so proud," Buddy said. "I'm honored to know you."

"Me, too," Skootch said.

"It was about you, too, Buddy. I was sure you were dead, and that was his fault just as sure as Mac and Howie, because if he hadn't killed Mac, you never would have been at risk. I was determined to get him. When he hit Juanita, I felt he had killed everything I loved. I became ..."

"He was a macho avenger." Dora batted her lashes, and her hips swayed ever so slightly.

"Our own Zorro," Buddy said.

"Stop it." Javier got up and paced the edge of the pool. "Seeing you. This is my real reward, *amigo*."

"And finding you, makes my world absolutely perfect." Buddy did a big back roll, sticking his curly piano legs into the air and doing the silly air dance of joy.

# Chapter 23

The household of Deedee Holmes and her daughter Maxine was everything a dog could wish for. If there was a rating system for pooch-friendly accommodations, the Holmes abode would have received five stars.

Buddy and Skootch each had his own bed at the foot of the big sleigh bed in Deedee's room. The dogs enjoyed breakfast in the kitchen at the same time the humans ate. Buddy had a matching set of blue bowls, and Skootch had a set of red ones.

After breakfast, Maxine took the dogs for a walk around the neighborhood before she went to work. In the afternoon, if it was not too hot in the desert, Deedee took them for another walk. On hot days, she drove them to the city's dog park for a romp under the shade trees.

At first, Skootch had been standoffish. He was more than willing to answer questions about proper indoor dog behavior and the finer points of canine etiquette, but Buddy thought Skootch would never allow him to be a friend.

As fall melted into winter, the temperature dropped and the dogs became more active. There were rabbits to chase and road-runners to surprise. Besides, there were the roof rats to keep at bay. They were attracted to Deedee's yard because of all the yummy fruit trees.

When Skootch was chasing rats, he let down his guard. Through activities like rat patrol, Buddy came to understand that

Skootch was a sweet old curmudgeon, a heart of gold wrapped in ebony ears and head-to-toe pointer dog ticking.

"Head him off, Buddy. Go around the pool!" Skootch scrambled left to herd the rat across the lawn. "Don't let him near the lemon tree."

The lemon tree was the route to the telephone pole and a short leap to the neighbor's yard. Buddy bounded off the patio, around the spa at the shallow end and down the length of the pool on the far side. "Gotcha, you thieving varmint." The rat's eyes nearly popped out of its head at the sight of the big white apparition bearing down on him.

The rat spun and made for Skootch. He faked a left and, once Skootch had committed himself, dodged right toward the grapefruit tree.

"Stop him, Bud, he'll escape to the roof." Skootch skidded to a stop at the edge of the deep end.

Buddy galloped toward the tree. The rat gained the trunk and started his climb toward the leafy boughs and safety. Buddy reached the tree as the creature made it to the first limb. The poodle stood on his hind legs and strained to reach the rat. He could almost touch his nose to the limb where the rat was clinging, so the rat leaped to the next highest branch.

"I'm afraid you've lost him." Skootch approached and sat down, winded.

"Not so fast." Buddy put his big paws against the tree trunk and pressed hard. The tree shook, the back legs of the rat slipped from the limb. The creature swung, his feet flailing in space.

Buddy pushed the trunk rhythmically until the whole tree was shaking.

"Ha, look! There are more of them!" Skootch got up. The chatter of angry rodents could be heard above the soft rustle of leaves. "You've got him this time!"

Grinning, Buddy gave the trunk another shove, putting his back into it. The first rat squealed, his grip slipping.

Skootch frowned, focusing on a thumping sound high in the tree. He gasped when he saw it. A monster grapefruit fell in the crotch of the tree, bounced and landed square on Buddy's forehead. The big dog fell back in a heap, sending a hail of dust and sand into the air.

Knowing his moment, the rat alighted on the lower limb, regained his footing and rocketed up the trunk to the roof. He was followed by two compatriots, their fat haunches swaying with the movement of the branch.

Buddy righted himself, spitting sand. His ears were festooned with leaves, sticks, and bits of bark.

Skootch couldn't help it. He tried to hide his snickers, by rubbing his nose with his paws.

"I thought I had him, Skootch." Buddy crossed his paws, dejected.

"Don't feel bad, big fella. You'll get another chance." In control of himself again, the older dog came over to Buddy and nuzzled his shoulder. "Let's go bark at crows."

The two companions sauntered off toward the other side of the yard where a mound of dirt near the pool equipment afforded an excellent view of the empty lot next door.

# Chapter 24

I reconciled myself to living in Paradise Valley, or rather I convinced everyone I had. There was no choice. A deal was a deal. I had given my word to the Good Shepherd, and, as Howie constantly reminded me, Sonny had delivered Buddy from his terrible existence and horrific death to an idyllic life of love and service in the Holmes household. No dog deserved it more.

Howie and I monitored Buddy's progress frequently. It did my heart good to see how Buddy took to his new life. He found joy in every little thing, but then, that was the kind of guy he was. Special.

Haven was a magnificent place, I had to admit, but it had way too many rules. The biggest rule of all was the Rule of Equi. It goes like this: Dogs spend a lifetime being man's best friend. We are man's protector, guide, companion, sometimes, even their savior, but when we die, our subservience comes to an end. Haven is the special part of Paradise Valley set aside for dogs. In Haven, we lack for nothing, make our own decisions, and, most importantly, we perform no work for humans.

Sonny explained the whole thing to me. He was a Big Cheese in Haven, with the important job of orienting new arrivals. Some of us took more orienting than others. I was a hard case.

I had heard that all dogs went to heaven, but I was a born skeptic. Who could believe such a thing?

Sonny was all patience. "You see, MacKenzie, humans have free will. It is a mystery why any human would hurt a dog, but some do. Such people go through the crack in the earth and cross the Bitter Sea to the Island of Lovelessness."

I thought of Kurtz. "Sounds fair."

"Dogs do not have free will. Their love of humans means they always act in the human's interest and not their own. In recognition of this sacrifice, all dogs, especially those who are mistreated, and even those who have behaved badly, are welcome in Haven. However, and I cannot stress this sternly enough, to maintain the cosmic balance, dogs must not intervene in the affairs of humans in Paradise Valley, or back on earth."

This sounded too good to be true, but I played along. "So that is why you had to get permission to implement Howie's suggestion."

"Exactly," the shepherd said. "We were treading one very thin line."

Off to our left a Rhodesian Ridgeback materialized. The dog looked old and confused.

"Newcomer," Sonny said, and shook himself as if he had been for a swim. The white desert transformed itself into the plains of Africa. Sonny changed his direction and strolled toward the Ridgeback.

I followed along. "But where are the humans?"

"You'll find them just across the perimeter." Sonny indicated the distant mountains. "On the other side of the creatureless void."

"But I can't get to the mountains." I started to get frustrated again. The perimeter was on the other side of the mountains.

"You'll get there when you learn to use your wings."

I took to practicing in a shallow ravine. Although I would rather have been alone, Howie would tag along. He would sit on a rock and exercise his wing muscles the way humans lift weights, up, down, up, down.

"Your landings are improving," he said.

"Thanks for nothing." I did a little hop and floated down, landing on one paw a few feet from him.

"MacKenzie, you're sharp, like all the Border Collies. It's amazing how much of this you have picked up on your own." Howie stepped off the rock and came over. "But there are subtleties."

"So?"

"So, you are not going to pass the test and become a full-fledged Havenite until you take the course."

"Nothing doing."

"But you're missing out."

"What do you mean?"

"It's not about getting to reach the perimeter."

"What's it about then, jughead?"

"It's about going beyond."

"Beyond the perimeter?" He had my attention. "Like, back to earth?"

"You bet. You'd get assigned missions, Mac." Howie's feet were dancing, his feathers swaying with the moves. "It's so you!"

"What are you talking about?"

Howie was bursting. "Haven dogs have one job left to do. We are responsible for guiding our own kind to their celestial home and seeing to it that their transition goes smoothly. You would be so good at it, but you have to pass the test."

"Nobody guided me to Haven." I had him there.

"Yes, they did."

"Who?"

He smiled his patient smile. "Me."

"But I don't remember ..."

"My choice." He rubbed my muzzle. "You always want things on your own terms, so I kind of kept out of your way."

I leaned away and glared at him. Howie's under lip wrinkled. His eyes grew moist. He knew me so well. In his laid-back way, he was always sensitive to my needs.

I rubbed his muzzle in turn. "It sounds a lot like herding."

# Chapter 25

Maxine let Buddy off his leash. Skootch, already freed, had made his way to the edge of the vast inland sea. The smell of dead fish overwhelmed his nostrils. Buddy broke into a trot to catch up with Skootch.

Maxine liked to hike. She wore a big floppy hat, and carried a special stick with a point on the end, two big bottles of water, a special cup so she could pour water for the dogs, and a box on a string around her neck. Every so often, she would stop, hold the box to her face and press a round button on its side.

Skootch was snuffling a pile of rotting fish when Buddy caught up with him. The older dog extended his tongue and pressed it against the fish on top of the pile. "Ugh, too old. Too bad."

Buddy tested the breeze. "Let's go to the other side. We can still run along the water, but we'll be upwind."

"Good idea. Just don't go too fast," Skootch said. "I'm not getting any younger."

Maxine had the box up in front of her face when the two dogs passed by going in the other direction. She dropped the box and squinted in the distance at the mountains, her hand over her eyes.

On the other side of the salty lake, the fish smell was much reduced. The dogs got wind of other scents, including the sweet smell of rabbits.

A rangy male jackrabbit broke from the protection of a creosote bush and accelerated over the dune.

"Hot diggity," Skootch yelled, and he was off.

"Don't injure yourself. Those dunes can be tricky." Buddy could have passed the older dog, but hung back because the jackrabbit was Skootch's find.

The dogs sailed over the dune, skidded down the other side, and followed the footprints of the rabbit as it rocketed over the sand.

They rounded another dune, powered through a ravine and ran across a mesa. Sides heaving, Skootch slowed to a trot. "I'd better give it up. You go ahead."

"I'll just check around the next dune. We may have lost him." Buddy loped away.

Buddy passed between two low dunes and descended into another ravine. "He's probably gone to ground."

Buddy stood still and listened. Bird and insect sounds dominated, although he thought he heard the subtle shush of a snake gliding over sand.

Ahead at a turn in the ravine, a shadow appeared. Buddy tensed. It might be a coyote.

A dog emerged from the shadows and staggered in Buddy's direction. As he drew nearer, Buddy could see that the dog was sickly. His bones showed, not just the ribs on his sides, but his shoulder blades and hip bones protruded under his hide. His lips were white, and his eyes looked cloudy.

The dog stopped in front of Buddy, swaying as if he might collapse any minute.

"You don't look too good, Bubb. When did you eat last?"

The dog looked confused. "Eat? That's a tough one. Last couple of days, I've had trouble remembering things. Comes and goes."

"Do you remember your name?"

"I'm called Leroy."

"You had better follow me, Leroy," Buddy said. "You need help."

It was slow going. The brown and white dog was in a very bad way. He could only take a few steps before having to stop and catch his breath. They made it out of the ravine and back to the two dunes when Leroy had to sit down.

"Don't you worry, I'll be right back." Buddy hurried along. He gained the mesa and spotted Skootch heading his way.

"What have you been doing?" the older dog said.

"Come quick," Buddy said, and swung back the way he'd come.

When the two dogs reached the brown and white dog, he was lying on his side, gulping air in rasping gasps.

Skootch sized up the situation. "He's almost done for."

The dog raised his head and looked at Skootch. "Dad?"

"He's delirious," Buddy said.

"Fast as you can Buddy. Get Maxine."

Maxine dragged the dog to her station wagon, using her work shirt. They went straight to the vet. The vet said Leroy had a life-threatening infection, the kind you pick up from the desert sands if you are weak and unlucky. He took a sample of Leroy's blood. He would not know what medicine to give Leroy until the blood was analyzed. Until he knew, he could only keep Leroy comfortable, nourished, and hydrated.

Buddy studied the sickly dog in the cage in the vet's hospital ward. "We'll be back for you tomorrow, Leroy. You must rest now."

"Thank you for all you have done, Buddy." Leroy spoke without lifting his head from the pallet. A tube ran from his leg to a bag dangling from a hook.

"How did you end up out there, all alone?" Skootch asked.

"I wasn't alone, at first," Leroy said, a tear running off his muzzle. "My brother and sister were with me. We were brought to the sea in the trunk of a car, and chased out into the desert."

"What happened to your siblings?" Buddy asked.

"My brother got weak and a coyote got him. My sister just curled up and died. I stayed with her, until she was cold." Leroy's lip trembled.

"Rest now. You are safe," Skootch said. "Come on, Bud, let him sleep."

The two dogs returned to the waiting room, where Maxine talked with the woman at the counter.

"Do you think he'll be alive in the morning?" Buddy asked.

"He has a chance, which is more than he had in the wild," Skootch said. "You gave him that chance. Let us hope it is enough."

Just before Christmas, Leroy Brown Straydog became Leroy Holmes. He came home from the hospital, and Maxine bought him a snappy purple collar that set off his liver brown spots. She also got him a shiny tag with his name and the Holmes phone number, just like Skootch and Buddy had. Never again would he be lost and alone. Deedee bought him some toys, and she did not wait for Christmas to give him the presents.

Skootch sat on the patio watching Leroy shake the funny green octopus. "He's a new dog, that's for sure."

"He's a lot younger than we thought. Just a kid really. When I found him, he was like an old man." Buddy observed Leroy from a safe distance. If Leroy started running around the pool again, the kid might run into him. "That medicine worked a miracle cure."

"He's having a second childhood." Skootch ducked out of the way as Leroy caromed past, the green toy's arms flapping on either side of his mouth. "Watch out, you maniac!"

Leroy circled the flowerbed, returned to the patio and dropped the toy in front of Skootch. "Sorry, Uncle Skootch, you wanna play with it?"

"My bones ache just thinking about it! Be more careful, okay?"

Leroy snatched the toy and took off.

"It is like watching a fury whirlwind." Buddy crossed his big paws. "It is nice to be called 'Uncle.' Remember the first day, when he called you 'Dad'?"

"Perfectly understandable," Skootch said. "He's a diversity dog. His daddy looked like me, and his mama like something else."

"What, do you think?"

"That's easy. See how his fur looks less like ticking than distinct spots?"

"Yes, I've noticed that."

"His mom was a Dalmatian. We'll need to be careful if he is taken for a walk. If a fire engine goes by, he'll give chase. Won't be able to help it."

Leroy shot past, carrying a stick, ears snapping, tail high.

"Can't watch anymore. Too exhausting." Skootch got up and walked toward the sliding door to the kitchen.

Buddy watched the younger dog as he flew along the far side of the pool. "Leroy is a happy dog, but I am the happiest dog of all. It feels good to pass it forward."

# Chapter 26

"Now you see 'em. Now, you don't." I demonstrated to Howie that I had mastered the ability to make my wings disappear when I wasn't using them. We were standing on a windy bluff overlooking an expanse of gray-green water. Two Chesapeake Bay Retrievers had arrived that morning, and Sonny had changed the scenery to make them feel welcome.

Howie grinned. "I am not surprised you graduated at the head of your class."

"When I set my mind to something, I achieve it." I unveiled my wings in a flourish, to emphasize my point.

"Show-off."

"Stop stalling, Howie. What's our first assignment?"

"It is a big one. You should be honored. It shows what confidence Sonny has in you."

"Come on, talk."

"We are to go to a shelter in Bakersfield. The authorities raided a farm and found dozens of neglected dogs. Ten are in such poor condition, they are to be euthanized. You and I are to be there for them, to bring them to Haven."

"This is big."

"Are you ready?"

My chest swelled with the knowledge I was once again in a position to help my fellow canines. I thought of Buddy, and smiled. "Am I ever!"

# Chapter 27

Buddy and Leroy sat on the knoll that overlooked the empty lot. A roadrunner was searching for bugs, and the bird's darts and thrusts were very entertaining.

"I could chase him," Leroy's eyes fixed on the bird, his tongue dangling.

"Control yourself. He has a right to hunt, just like us." Buddy gave Leroy's shoulder a loving bump. He had calmed down in the two years he had lived with the Holmeses, but he still had more energy than a bevy of foxhounds.

Leroy's tongue snapped back into his mouth and his ears perked. "Hey, who's that?"

Buddy saw the movement, too. A dog huddled behind a scraggly bush at the rear of the lot. She leaned her neck forward and peaked at the street, but when a car hurried by, she snatched her head back and cowered behind the bush.

"She looks lost," Leroy said.

"And something more." Buddy looked over his shoulder at his house. Skootch, Deedee, and Maxine were inside. "I'll pop over and see if she needs anything."

"You sure?" Leroy was surprised. Deedee did not like the dogs to go into the neighborhood without human supervision. Buddy and Leroy respected her wishes, even though there was a storage bin for hoses that served as a dandy launch pad for getting over the wall.

"This looks like an emergency." Buddy descended from the knoll and approached the bin. "You be lookout."

With his long legs, jumping over the wall was the easiest thing in the world. Buddy trotted across the lot and approached the trembling female.

"Hello, my name is Buddy, and I live over there." He sat at a respectable distance. This lady was a bundle of nerves.

The dog looked at him, at the street and back at him. She shrunk into the shadows.

"You seem to be hiding from someone. Is it okay if I come back there? I don't want to call attention to you." Buddy waited for her reply. She stared at him so long, he was sure she would refuse.

The dog nodded, and moved further back to make room for him. Buddy moved behind the bush and stretched out on the sand. At closer range, Buddy could see that the dog had long welts on her rump. She also had a gash on her muzzle. She held her tail firmly between her legs as if she were expecting to be scolded at any moment.

"What's your story?" Buddy tilted his head and adopted an encouraging smile.

"I'm running away."

"Somebody beat you." Buddy nodded toward the dog's injured hip.

"And he will again, if he finds me."

"But why?" Buddy had been neglected, but Mr. Swindell never struck him. Well, almost never, and only with his palm.

"He is a stupid failure of a man, but that means he has no one to lord it over except an animal." After checking to make sure her head would not show, the dog sat up. "My name is Roxanne."

"You're a diversity dog. What breeds are you?"

"I'm half German Shorthaired Pointer, one quarter German Shepherd and one quarter Greyhound."

Buddy thought Skootch's kind really got around. "You are a very pretty combination, if you don't mind my saying so."

"I can run and I can hunt. I'm counting on that to get away from my master." Roxanne stole a look around the bush.

"It's okay. I'll watch the street for you. Relax."

Roxanne let out a big sigh in an attempt to follow Buddy's advice.

"Have you eaten today?"

"No. I didn't have anything yesterday either. I'm afraid to go where people are. Someone might recognize me. Tonight I will head for the desert. I will be safe there."

Buddy thought of the fate that claimed Leroy's sister and brother. "I've got a better idea. Come home with me. I'll get you a good meal."

"No, I couldn't. Your people might turn me in."

"Not when they see your wounds."

"No, I'm too afraid."

"Then I will bring something to you. Wait here."

Buddy bounded toward the wall, gathering speed. On this side, there was no bin to jump on, but there was plenty of wide open space to build momentum. At the right moment, he went airborne.

Leroy almost jumped into the pool when the big dog landed near him.

"Come on, Leroy, we've got a mission." Bud trotted to the doggie door. He entered the kitchen and nosed open the bin containing the dog food. He took the tin cup Deedee used as a scoop, filled it with kibble and dumped the kibble in his bowl.

"What are you doing, Bud? It isn't dinnertime." Skootch rolled to an upright position as Buddy went back for another scoop.

Buddy dumped the food in the bowl. "There's a young girl in trouble in the vacant lot. I'm going to take her food."

109

"How are you going to manage it?"

"I'm going to jump over the wall with the bowl in my mouth. I know I will spill some, but some food will make it."

Leroy came up beside him. "This is exciting."

"The thing I can't figure out is how to get water to her."

With an effort, Skootch pushed up on his haunches. His brow wrinkled and he snorted. "I think I might have an idea. Leroy, bring your bowl."

The three dogs headed down the hallway in a procession with Buddy in the lead. Deedee was in the living room reading the paper. She lowered the paper in time to see Leroy's rump and a determined Skootch disappear through the alcove.

The three dogs studied the wall.

Skootch, who had positioned himself on the knoll, turned to Buddy. "I think it's all in the landing. If you touch down and just keep running, you'll lose the least amount of kibble."

Buddy got a firm grip on the bowl. Fortunately, he had a very large mouth. He walked to the far end of the pool so that he could put on enough speed before he hit the hose bin, giving himself the smoothest trajectory. He lifted his head high and took off.

The food shifted when he executed the spring from the bin, but he only lost a few kernels. He sailed over the wall, his front feet touched ground, and, just as Skootch had suggested, he kept going.

The food lifted in the air off the bottom of the bowl, but he keep the dish under it and it settled back down. Trying not to grin at his success for fear he would drop his prize, Buddy slowed his pace.

Roxanne had watched the whole thing. Her face was a study in amazement as he reached the bush and placed the bowl in front of her.

"I hope you like it. It's chicken and bacon flavor."

110

"Oh, my." Roxanne gaped at the dish.

"Go on, it's not going to bite you. Besides, if you don't eat fast, the ants will get in the food. I hate that." Buddy shivered in distaste.

Roxanne put her head to the bowl and took a dainty taste.

"Good," Buddy said. "I'll be back. I'm going to see what I can do about water."

As Buddy neared the wall, Leroy flew over carrying his bowl. He dropped the bowl, circled Buddy still running, and made for the wall. "Skootch is so smart. Wait 'til you see."

Before Buddy could answer, Leroy soared back over the wall. Puzzled, he sat down. He could hear scuffling and grunting on the other side.

When he heard the pound of paws on the pool deck, he started to rise. Leroy leaped over the wall with a section of garden hose between his teeth. He landed well, but was pulled off his feet because the other end of the hose hung up on something.

Leroy spat the hose on the ground and gasped for breath. "Phew."

Buddy nuzzled the younger dog who, for once, looked worn out. "What gives?

"Skootch is going to turn on the hose. He says he can turn the valve with his teeth."

"I'll get the bowl." Buddy retrieved Leroy's bowl and placed it under the nozzle. A trickle of water dripped into the bowl.

"Maybe I'd better go see how he is doing." Leroy turned.

"No. Leave him be. He knows what he's about."

Heads together, the two dogs watch the thin stream, willing it to grow. Behind them the hose shifted and a low gurgling noise rose from the tube. They leaned closer.

The nozzle hissed, rose from the edge of the bowl like a snake, and sprayed the dogs with a blast of cold water. Buddy jumped

111

back, his topknot dripping in all directions. Soaked and laughing, Leroy shook and splashed Buddy again.

"Stop that, you dolt. Get that hose. Sneak up on it from the back!"

Leroy did as he was told, gripped the hose, and angled it over the water bowl.

When the bowl was full, Buddy carried it to Roxanne.

"This is very kind of you, Buddy," Roxanne said between sips. "I hope your fur dries before the sun sets."

"I'll be okay. Won't you consider spending the night with us?"

"No, I just can't."

Buddy's shoulders fell. He moped back to where Leroy waited. Skootch must have turned off the water, because the hose lay still and innocent on the ground. "You first, kid."

Leroy took the wall. Buddy heard him land and took off himself. He would pull the hose back over the wall after he landed.

Buddy hit the grass and trotted a half dozen steps before he came to a halt.

"What have you been up to, Mr. B.?" Deedee stood with her hands on her hips, her foot tapping. Skootch, his head hanging in disgrace, sat by the dripping spigot in a circle of hose. "I went to fix your dinner and there weren't any bowls. What is going on here?"

Leroy's eyes darted to the hose, where it rose and disappeared over the wall.

Deedee walked to the wall and squinted into the growing twilight. She scanned the lot, and her head stopped turning opposite the bush. "Ah, we have a squatter, I see."

She looked at her trio of dogs. "Stay. I'll be back."

Deedee returned from the house with three large milk bones. She bent and held them out to Buddy. "Perhaps it will be easier to carry these over, than a bowl full of kibble."

# Chapter 28

Sonny grunted and spun in a circle. A cyclone of sand rose around the shepherd, crystallizing and winking in the light. The landscape shimmied and big blue-green fir trees exploded from the ground like a row of growing whiskers.

I blinked, and all I could see in every direction was snow, snow, and more snow. The frozen surface rolled and glistened pink and blue.

"These winter landscapes are hard work." Sonny collapsed on his haunches. "I'm expecting a team of Siberian Huskies. There was an unfortunate blizzard during the Iditarod."

"The what?" I shook crystals from my coat.

"Never mind. Let's talk about your next assignment."

"I'm all ears, if they don't freeze up on me."

"Your next mission involves a puppy mill. Some little ones are going to die. There are too many of them in the cage."

"Terrible."

"I agree," Sonny said. "Now, don't get this wrong, Mac. You are a fantastic guide and transition dog, no question, but I'm going to send a partner along with you on this one."

"What?" I jumped up. I did not need a partner. "I haven't had a partner since my training."

"I'm aware of that."

"So, what's the problem?"

"You're a single lady, right?"

"Yeah, what's your point?"

"My point is, you know nothing about puppies."

I was speechless. True, I had never had a litter, but that was because I was a career girl. There had been no time for dating at the golf course.

"I've found the perfect dog to accompany you to the puppy mill."

"Okay, I'll bite. Who's the lucky woman?"

"Your mother."

Stunned, my mind reeled. I saw my litter, squirming in a fluffy bundle, each roly-poly one of us trying to reach a nipple. I felt my mother's breath on my tummy as Mom nudged me forward so I could nurse. My heart beat so hard I could feel the throbs in my ears. "Mom's here?"

"Of course."

"Why haven't I seen her before?"

"She's been waiting for you to ask for her."

I remembered my anguished yelps when I was taken away to be trained. As the handler placed me in the crate, I howled, reproaching my mother. "Why must I go? Why am I the first?"

My body stiffened with the memory. "We had a difficult leave-taking."

"So she said." Sonny turned and faced east. The ascending sun backlit an approaching figure, throwing a long shadow across the glistening snow.

"Hello, MacKenzie. You look fit." My mother walked up the rise where Sonny and I were resting and sat next to me. She looked just as I remembered, her delicate muzzle, slightly thinner than most Border Collies, was dusted with a coat of powdery snow. The glossy black portion of her abundant fur glowed blue in the sunlight.

I drank in her scent, almost falling over with the recognition of its sweet power. "Mom, you look—you are just the way you were the day I left."

"Flattery will take you far." Mom sidled a little closer.

"Jean, it's easy to see the family resemblance. Your ears are interchangeable."

"She was my only girl in that litter. Everyone spoiled her."

"I'm sure the two of you have a lot of catching up to do, so I'll get to the point." Sonny filled us in on our task. We were to bring two Cocker Spaniel puppies to Haven. The babies were barely weaned, so making them feel safe would require all my mother's considerable skill.

Sonny looked up. A team of eight Huskies materialized at the bottom of the hill, accompanied by Pierre, a very experienced St. Bernard escort. The dogs were still in their harness.

"Wise move on Pierre's part," Sonny said, pointing to the gear. "That rig makes them feel comfortable. It's what they know."

"How will he get it off them?" I asked.

"It will evaporate as soon as they feel secure enough not to need it. I've got to go greet them. You have any more questions?"

"We're good, Sonny," Jean said.

Sonny nodded, unfurled his wings and glided down to the Huskies.

Mom and I materialized in the backyard of a low, mean building that stretched along the edge of Route 10 in San Bernardino. Waves of grit-filled air blew from the busy freeway and settled on the scruffy dirt of the yard.

"What an awful place. Look at those pens." Mom indicated a row of narrow, filthy runs jutting from the back of the building.

"These guys need to be shut down." A low growl came from my throat as a fat man in a sweatshirt slammed the door and headed for a pickup truck, hefting two carriers.

"The time for our mission has not come yet, so we will have to wait. Let's sit over there in the shade. The building will be between us and the freeway."

We made small talk for a while. Mom talked of my siblings. I told her about Buddy, my final confrontation with the evil Hummer driver, and Javier's bravery. Finally, we got around to my issues.

"You were the fastest learner, child, my brightest, my greatest achievement," Mother said. "It was your destiny to go first."

"I should not have said what I did to you. It was childish of me."

"You were a child. You said what you felt," Mother sighed. "You were forgiven long ago. It is a hard world, and we are working dogs."

"Yes, we have responsibilities." I saw myself running on the fairway at the golf course, racing the wind.

"There is a time to be weaned, and a time to train, a time to work, and a time to rest." My mother lifted her nose and sniffed. "A time to run, and a time to lie down. Come, the children are ready for us now."

We melted through the wall of the building, and walked down a row of cages stacked three high, packed chock full with dogs of every breed. The raucous barking was made up of every kind of message—anger, fear, longing, boredom, regret, and even love.

As we reached the cage with the Cocker puppies, two tiny souls rose from two still ebony bodies.

"Come here, children," Mom said. "Come and get a kiss."

# Chapter 29

It took two nights and three days to entice Roxanne over the wall into the Holmes yard. At first she hid behind the pool equipment whenever Deedee or Maxine came outside. Deedee found Roxanne a pair of extra bowls, and Maxine brought out some old blankets, folded them in quarters, and placed them in a corner of the porch.

After a week Roxanne was able to tolerate Deedee and Maxine, perhaps because they were women like her. Deedee was even able to stroke Roxanne's head and rub her special place next to her chin.

There was one awful day, when the pool man arrived early, catching Roxanne out, before she had time to hide under the chaise lounge. He wore sturdy boots, carried a long aluminum pole with a net on the end, and was very tall. Roxanne retreated over the wall, and when Buddy found her in her old spot behind the bush, she had wet herself.

It took Buddy an entire month of coaxing to lure Roxanne through the doggie door and into the house. Trembling, she investigated every room, and settled on a darkened corner of Maxine's office as her place. Maxine retrieved her blankets and placed them in the spot. Roxanne's bowls were moved to the kitchen beside Leroy's bowls.

The following week, Deedee came home with new bowls, a proper dog bed, and a pink collar with sequins. Everyone told Roxanne how pretty she looked in pink. The Holmes clan had a new member.

"Wait for it. Wait for it, Leroy." Skootch stood poised at the edge of the pool, rocking from paw to paw.

The roof rat, hanging upside down on the tree trunk, had one foot on the ground. The creature studied the orange tree on the other side of the birdbath, trying to decide if he could make it.

Leroy's muscles rippled. If he leaned any further forward, he was going to fall in the flowerbed.

"Easy, Leroy. Roxanne, stand your ground." Skootch spoke, never taking his eyes off the rat.

"Maybe, if we flushed him," Roxanne said.

"Nothing doing. He'd just go back up the tree." Buddy watched the proceedings. He wasn't keen on rat chasing, even though he was very good at it. Better to let the youngsters have the practice.

The rat dropped to the ground and made a beeline for the orange tree. Leroy and Roxanne exploded into action. Roxanne powered down the gap between the flowers and the wall, preventing the rat's escape up the stucco surface and over into the neighbor's yard. Leroy bore down on the creature, reaching him just as he cleared the birdbath.

"Gotcha!" Leroy rolled the rat and grabbed him around the middle.

"Good work, boy!" Skootch approached from the rear.

"Ouch!" Leroy jumped. The creature had him by the muzzle, scratching with his claws. The rat reared back and sunk his teeth into Leroy's nose.

Leroy shook his head, but the thing hung on, biting harder. Leroy rolled back, snapped his head and flung the rat in the air.

The rat did a somersault, landing inches from Skootch. Surprised, the old dog shifted his body to reach for the rat, and his back legs went over the edge of the pool.

"No!" Roxanne screamed as Skootch disappeared under the water at the deep end.

Buddy, Leroy, and Roxanne ran to the edge of the tile and peered into the water.

"Can he swim?" Roxanne asked.

"He hasn't for years. His arthritis. Besides, he always stayed in the shallow part."

Skootch came to the surface, sputtering and splashing with his paws.

"He's a field dog, not a water retriever." Leroy paced the side of the pool. "He's not making any progress."

"He'll wear himself out," Roxanne said. "What can we do?"

"I have to help him." Buddy jumped into the water, his ears flying. "Skootch, I'm coming."

"Can't make it," Skootch's legs were slowing. "Joints are shot."

"Take it easy. I'm going to come up under you."

Buddy dove. The water around Skootch became opaque with bubbles and ripples.

"What do you think he's doing?" Leroy leaned over the edge, his muzzle almost in the water.

"He's going to pull Skootch to safety." Roxanne was still as a statue.

"Skootch is too heavy."

Buddy's head popped out of the water between Skootch's legs. "Hold on, old guy."

Exhausted, Skootch dropped his paws onto the big poodle's shoulders. Buddy began to dog-paddle. His big hind legs struck out, churning the turquoise water.

"This could work." Roxanne ran down the pool to the steps where Buddy was heading.

"Look, Skootch let go!" Leroy yelled.

Skootch sank below the surface. Buddy circled and dove again, coming up under the flailing dog. He pushed Skootch's chest up, and the pointer's head came out of the water.

"Sorry," Skootch sputtered. "Your shoulders are narrow and my paws slipped off."

Buddy was breathing hard with the effort. His heart pounded and his paws felt like lead. He eyed the steps. They seemed miles away.

"He's slowing, Roxanne. They both could drown."

"No, come down here, Leroy." Roxanne placed her paw on the first step and cringed. "We're not water dogs either, but we can do this."

Leroy reached her side and descended the steps until only his neck and head were above water. "Come guys, we're right here. You can do it."

Encouraged by their support, Buddy gave it everything he had. His front paws cut the water, sending fishtails along the surface. His back legs pumped.

"Let me go, man. It's too far." Skootch said in his ear.

"No way." Buddy gulped in air, and strained forward. The tip of his paw hit something.

"You've made it." In his excitement, Leroy fell off the last step and went under.

"Paw down, Buddy. The step is under you," Roxanne said.

Buddy placed both paws on the step and twisted his body so Skootch could reach the next tread. Buddy was the tallest, so the first step worked for him.

The four dogs sat in the water, waiting for Skootch to regain enough strength to get out of the pool.

"You saved my life, Bud. And my honor. Think about it. I could have gone down in history as the only dog ever drowned by a rat." Skootch looked over his shoulder. "Where is that mangy varmint?"

"I'd go to the ends of the earth for you, Skootch." Buddy cuffed the old dog on the shoulder.

Leroy fell off the step again when Deedee spoke behind them. "I see you kids have found a way to stay cool."

Deedee helped Skootch out of the pool and treated the dogs to a good rubdown with some old beach towels.

That evening, Skootch and Buddy lay in their dog beds, noses inches from each other.

"When I was fighting to get to the surface, I saw a light. Not the light above the water, but something else. It was peaceful. You ever experience anything like that?" Skootch asked.

Buddy pictured himself observing his own body in that other pool so long ago. "Sort of."

"What do you think it means?"

"I think it means that we shouldn't be afraid."

# Chapter 30

Howie and I strolled along the perimeter of Haven. We were on the human side of the valley, and across the fog-filled, creatureless void between their wall and ours, we could see people going about their business.

"So, if we don't guide the humans to Paradise Valley, who does?" I studied our wall. It was an ornate affair, rendered in a bone motif.

"Who cares? It's their problem." Howie sniffed the close clipped grass of the Troon golf course. Sonny was expecting a Scottish Terrier. We were all wearing plaid tams in greeting. The golf course scenery made me antsy. I felt I should be doing something.

"You know what a bad sense of direction they have. They couldn't follow a scent trail if their lives depended on it," I said.

"True, but it is none of our concern." Howie walked on. His aura of calm and content could be very irritating to a dog like me.

"Don't you ever question the setup here?" I speeded up and got in front of him.

Howie shrugged. "Why would I do that? I have everything I could ever want. More. I can fly. Imagine how useful that would have been in Yucca Dunes."

"That's it. Let's go make the black hole again, so we can look down and see how they're doing."

"We haven't done that in a while," Howie said. "Let's get Sonny." Howie trotted to a little hill and scanned the horizon for the Good Shepherd.

"No, don't bother with him. He's got that Scottie to cope with."

123

"I guess it will be okay." Howie turned around, and we headed toward the path to the plain where the black pond waited.

We reached the edge, and settled next to each other, paws dangling over the lip. I concentrated hard and bright colors began to rise from the gloom.

Buddy checked the place settings one more time. Skootch's fifteenth birthday party had to be perfect. Deedee had placed a milk bone at each place and a colorful little cup with bacon-flavored treats.

"They're here!" Leroy yelled.

Buddy followed Leroy to the gate. Derek trailed Javier into the yard. "Welcome, guys, glad you could make it."

"Is it a surprise?" Javier asked.

Buddy noticed the Chihuahua had gotten a little thick around the middle. Derek's feet had mellowed. Their original DayGlo orange hue was now a muted metallic copper.

"No, he's been informed," Buddy said. "I don't think it's a good idea to surprise a senior citizen."

When they returned to the table, Skootch was sitting in the place of honor. Deedee was perching a party hat on the birthday boy. She adjusted the elastic string under his chin.

Javier spoke to Buddy in a whisper. "Is Eliza bringing that cat?"

"Heavens, no! This is a dogs only event."

Maxine put a hat on Derek. The Rottweiler kept trying to see the hat, and his eyes crossed as he looked up.

Javier struggled into his seat, his eyes just high enough for him to see the cup of treats.

"What a minute, Skootch, you're not wearing the collar Deedee gave you."

"Oh, I forgot. Had my mind on the treats."

"No problem, I'll get it." Buddy bounded off, blasted through the doggie door, dashed down the hall, and skidded around the corner into Deedee's bedroom.

The gift was lying on a pile of shredded tissue paper. Skootch was ruthless when it came to opening packages. Buddy grabbed the collar and turned.

"Hello, Buddy."

Buddy dropped the collar. Curled in Deedee's big wing chair by the sleigh bed was the white shepherd.

Sonny sat up. "It's time."

Slowly, Buddy sat by the forgotten gift. "I don't believe it."

"Six years. Well, it will be six years, fifteen seconds from now."

"No. I mean, I believe you, but it ... The time has flown by."

"Of course it has. It is a loving home."

"Oh, yes. It was everything I imagined it would be. And more."

Sonny jumped down from the chair. "Ready?"

Buddy rose and walked to his side. He turned and saw himself lying on Deedee's Persian carpet, the gift collar resting next to his front paws.

Leroy dashed into the room. "What's taking so long, Buddy?"

He stopped in his tracks and stared. "Buddy?"

Leroy crept forward and touched his muzzle to Buddy's foot. "Buddy?"

He moved closer, placing his nose next to Buddy's nostrils and sniffed.

Leroy's lip quivered. Slowly he sat, lifting his head toward the ceiling. He pursed his lips and keened a high timeless reverberating howl, a sound so mournful, it could only have come from the deepest, most secret corners of his immortal canine soul.

# Chapter 31

Buddy took to guide duty like a trout to a sparkling stream. He was a natural, no question about it. He was better at it than I was, although no one in Haven would acknowledge this out loud because they know how competitive I am. Between you and me, though, he was the best. Patient, kind and thoughtful— that was Buddy all over.

Buddy looked very good in his wings. They seemed to suit him better than any dog in Haven. They were white as his fur, but pink underneath like his ears, and when he unfurled them, he looked elegant and noble like Pegasus.

I remember when he guided Skootch to Haven like it was yesterday.

"Mac, you'll never guess!" Buddy sprinted up to me and sat down with a plop. "Sonny is sending me for Skootch!"

"The old curmudgeon?"

"Yes. He's seventeen and his joints have given out. Hips are so bad, if he gets down, he can't get up. Heart's gonna fail any time now." Buddy was up again, pacing as he talked. "I'll be able to see Deedee again, and all the gang. Of course, they won't be able to see me."

Behind Buddy, the scenery started to shimmer. I sat up. "Oh, oh, Sonny's at it again."

"Wait 'til you see. I've asked for something special for Skootch."

Everything, as far as the eye could see, was green, although you couldn't see very far, because we were surrounded by trees.

"Wait a minute. You guys live in a desert. Yucca Dunes is dry, parched to a crisp."

"But Deedee's yard is full of plants and trees. Skootch is especially fond of orange trees, because that is where the rats hang out. That dog loves to chase varmints."

"So this is …"

"An orange grove. Why fool around with one piddling tree, when you can have an orchard?"

"Buddy, you are amazing."

"Looks like everything is ready. I had better get going." Buddy headed down the path between the trees. "Can you wait here? I'd like you to meet Skootch."

"I'll be here." I stretched out on a soft grassy patch and closed my eyes.

Buddy crept into the dark bedroom. Deedee snored softly in her big sleigh bed, her silver hair fanned on the pillow. Leroy lay on his back, his front feet bent at the wrists, his ears flopped open like petals.

Buddy would have liked to glide down the hall to Maxine's room and her office where Roxanne would be sleeping, but there wasn't time. Skootch was leaving his body.

The pointer rose from his bed, leaving his ancient head, drooping jowls, and twisted joints behind. The dog that emerged had a sleek ebony patch over one eye and ear without a trace of gray hair. His muscles were firm and his tummy flat.

"Come, Skootch, I've got a surprise for you."

"Buddy. My pal."

Buddy felt a particular joy when Skootch call him a pal. The two dogs turned to leave, but a shadow appeared in the doorway.

Roxanne took two steps into the room. She stopped and listened.

"Sometimes," Buddy said, "they sense our presence."

Buddy moved to Roxanne's side, and ever so gently licked her cheek.

Roxanne sighed a long, peaceful sigh. She walked to the spot between Skootch's body and the sleeping Leroy's, circled and lay down with her head on the edge of Leroy's bed.

"She'll be there to comfort him in the morning," Buddy said, fading into the night.

"Hot diggity dog." Skootch circled the orange trees, making a figure eight around the two nearest ones.

"Come here and meet Mac."

"I've heard a lot about you," Skootch said. He sat in front of us, but fell over backwards.

"It's the weight of the wings. You'll get used to it," I said.

Skootch righted himself. "I've been falling over a lot recently because my legs wouldn't work anymore. Compared to that, I'll take wings any day."

Buddy's fluff ball of a tail was spinning around the crazy way it did when he was very happy. "Haven is wonderful in so many ways, right Mac?"

I still had my reservations about Haven and all its rules, but I was not going to say anything that would spoil this day for my friend.

"It's special," I said. "Very special."

# Chapter 32

Sonny paced up to the edge of the precipice, stared into the rock strewn valley and returned to Buddy. "I don't know. Maybe it makes more sense to make the other landscape."

"What is this place?" Buddy asked.

"It is called Afghanistan. It is a hard land." Sonny cocked his head, thinking.

"What's the other choice?"

"Cornfields. Far as the eye can see. The Labrador Retriever you are assigned to collect grew up in Illinois, but he will die in Afghanistan down in a valley like that, on a dusty road to nowhere."

"So, you have to decide what will make him more comfortable, his immediate surroundings or his real home."

"Yes. It is always a difficult decision when a dog dies a violent death." Sonny squeezed his eyes together and shook his head. The cliff where they were sitting sank and the rocks evaporated. A rustling sound filled the air, and the dogs found that they were sitting on the edge of a gravel road that bisected two cornfields. The corn stalks swayed in the breeze.

"I'm liking the corn." Buddy crossed the ditch and sniffed an ear of yellow corn, the husk tickling his nose.

"You had better get moving. It is time," Sonny said.

When Buddy materialized in Afghanistan, he couldn't see a thing. After circling and sniffing, he realized he was standing in a bomb crater. The hole smelled of metal and fire. He hopped up on the rim and looked around.

He was on the edge of a rutted road. Thirty feet in front of him, a vehicle lay on its roof, smoking. It looked like the bad man's Hummer, except it wasn't black. Most of it was the color of desert sand, except for the parts where the paint had been scraped or burned off.

On the other side of the road were two more craters. As he started across the road, an explosion filled the air with rocks and dust. He could feel the concussion press against his body, and his ears roared in protest.

As the dust settled, he saw a black Labrador lying on his side in a field crisscrossed with tire tracks. Next to the dog's chest was a pool of blood, dusted over with debris.

Buddy approached the dog. To the right of the Lab was a soldier crawling toward the dog. The man's face was twisted in agony. "Badge. Badge!"

The man reached his hand out and the tips of his fingers touched the dog's fur. His lips parted in a weak smile. With an effort, he pulled himself across the remaining distance and rested His head on the lab's shoulder. Buddy realized the man could not see his dog, only feel him. He could not see the blood and the corpse was still warm, so he did not know his companion was dead.

Buddy saw the dog's soul start to emerge from its body and sink back in.

"Come on out, Badge. No point hesitating." Buddy found a spot to sit. "Nothing to fear now."

The man moaned. Buddy noticed he was missing a boot and his leg was soaked with blood.

"You have to go, Badge. You're work here is over."

"I can't leave him. He's my partner."

"Come out and sit with me."

Badge separated from his remains. He did not come to Buddy, but circled behind the man and sat as near to him as he could get. "We're United States Marines. I'm a bomb dog."

"I know. What happened here?"

"Ambush. Roadside bomb. This is as far as we got from the wreck."

Buddy looked back at the upturned vehicle. He thought he saw the outline of a still body in the rubble beside the driver's door. He looked back at the man between them, and the growing circle of blood by his leg.

"Your marine will not suffer much longer."

"I know." The dog hunkered down next to his comrade.

Buddy figured there would be no harm in waiting for the injured man to breathe his last. He settled onto the dusty ground. After the marine died, Badge would follow Buddy to Haven, comforted by the thought that he had done his duty to the end.

The dogs waited. The sun was setting and the sound of distant gunfire intensified. Buddy studied the horizon where a string of explosions competed with the sunset for color and brilliance.

The man's chest shuddered and his throat sounds became ragged chokes. A lonely whine escaped Badge's lips.

The marine's head tilted back, and his eyes although open, became as dead as river stones.

"He's gone." Buddy rose out of respect.

Badge placed his muzzle next to the marine's neck and inhaled the last faint traces of life smell. Then he got up and came to Buddy.

"I am your guide. I have come to take you to Haven, the paradise for dogs," Buddy said.

The two dogs walked to the road. Buddy made for a crest beyond the ruined transport. It would be a perfect place from which to say farewell to this valley of death and dematerialize.

"Badge? Badge!"

"Wait, he's coming!" Badge reversed direction and disappeared into the night.

"He can't come with us," Buddy said. "It's the rule."

Badge reappeared at the edge of the road. The man came out of the darkness, following the dog.

"No, no," Buddy said. "He has to wait for his own kind."

Badge closed the distance slowly. The marine was leaning on the dog.

Buddy had never encountered a situation like this before. There had never been any humans in the picture on his other missions, not dead humans anyway. Sonny had not prepared him for this.

I guess Sonny's not perfect, Buddy thought, as he tried to figure out his next move.

Badge and the marine looked at Buddy. "This is Andy," Badge said.

"Hello, Andy." Buddy saw the man respond to his bark. "My name is Buddy."

"Buddy," the man repeated.

He understands me. Maybe that is for the good, Buddy figured. Marines understand orders.

Buddy looked from Badge to Andy. "I have been sent to guide Badge to Haven. I'm sorry, but I am not permitted to escort you, only Badge."

"I see," Andy said, stroking Badge's head.

"I don't," Badge said. "Marines don't leave their comrades."

"Someone will come for him. One of his kind."

"Then we should wait." Badge sat.

The sounds of fighting were coming closer. Buddy could make out shouts and screams under the gunfire and explosions.

"Badge, you go ahead. I'm sure Buddy knows what he is talking about."

"Nothing doing." Badge was a statue. He didn't move a muscle when the big bombs exploded over the hill a few hundred yards away. Buddy thought that given the way things were going, this mission would turn out to be the longest on record.

The marine lowered himself to his hip, leaned on one hand and pulled his dog to him, his chin resting on Badge's forehead. "He's always had a stubborn streak."

Buddy sat on the road. He had never thought to ask Sonny what sort of procedure the humans used. They must send a guide. It was the sensible thing to do.

The poodle turned and jumped aside. A convoy of rusty vehicles flew over the crest of the road and down toward their position. There was a big flatbed truck, two vans and a pickup. A man in the back of the flatbed was trying to aim a long tube at what was coming behind them, but he could not keep his footing.

The vehicles flashed by, and another, larger convoy gained the crest. Three armored vehicles roared past, the first with its machine gun firing. Traces sliced the night sky. The driver of one of the vans lost control, and the van slid off the road and flipped down the slope into a ravine.

A knot of men with rifles struggled to exit from the van as it lay on its side. The hatch on the nearest armored vehicle burst open and a helmet emerged.

The marine pointed up to the turret and smiled. "Things are going to get hot."

"We've got to get out of here," Buddy looked at Badge.

"Says you." Badge continued to sit.

"I'm your guide. I must bring you home." Buddy moved to the left, out of the way of the advancing marines.

"How's his guide going to find him in this firefight?" Badge had risen to his feet, his legs stiff and his jaw set.

Buddy cringed as another detonation rocked the closest vehicle. Burning debris fell from the sky like hail. "Okay, he can come. Move it."

Buddy lead Badge and Andy to the crest. They turned to face the battle one last time. The fighters were backlit by flames from the van, which was completely engulfed.

Buddy made the circle of oneness around the man and the dog, then sat so that his body touched both of them.

*"Semper Fi,* guys," Badge said, as the three dissolved into crystals that sifted down to the ground and faded to match the native sand.

# Chapter 33

"This is so cool!" Badge ran down the long row of corn.

Buddy tried to keep up, but he was taller and was hit in the face with more leaves. Badge shot out of the cornfield and waited on the road for Buddy to emerge. Buddy hopped over the ditch, sat, and swatted at his ears to get the silk out of his fur.

A hazy pinpoint far down the rod straight road started to grow. "That will be Sonny," Buddy said, calling Badge's attention to the moving dot.

The cornstalks nearest the road shuddered, the gravel on the road danced a little jig, and Sonny came to a screeching stop before them.

"Are those wings?" Badge got a look at the shepherd's sparkling pair before he folded them away. "If I had those, I could apply for flight duty."

"Welcome to Haven, Badge. We are always honored when the brave dogs come home."

"Sonny, there, ah, might be a bit of a problem ..."

The corn along the row the dogs had come down began to rustle. The three dogs studied the waving tassels.

Andy parted the last of the stalks and stood smiling on the far side of the ditch.

"He can't be here." Sonny spun around so hard, his wings came unfurled. "Buddy, what have you done?"

"We didn't mean to get anybody in trouble," Badge said.

"You didn't know. It was for Buddy to set you straight." Sonny glared at his star guide, or his former star from the look of things.

"I didn't know what to do, Sonny." Buddy hung his head and his ears fell forward. "Nobody came for him."

"It is for humans to look after humans. And dogs to look after dogs." Sonny's voice was stern, and his eyes were hard. "Battle or no battle, the man was beyond harm. You should have seen that and done your duty."

"But Andy would have been alone," Badge looked confused.

Sonny's voice softened. "Your duty to Andy ended with your life. Now, you are here, you will learn about the rules. The Rule of Equi is not to be broken. Buddy knew that, even if you did not."

Sonny gave one flap of his wings and glided over the ditch. "We will walk Andy to the perimeter. I will help him over our wall and across the creatureless void. From there on, it is up to him. I have no idea what comes of such an unorthodox arrival in human paradise."

As he entered the corn, the stalks seemed to recede, making a path for the Good Shepherd.

Buddy brought up the rear of the forlorn procession. Just as surely as the corn had opened for Sonny, the stalks came back together after Buddy, like jaws snapping at a bone.

As Andy said his goodbyes to Badge, a small crowd of us dogs gathered at a distance. We could hear the murmurings rise and fall on the breeze. I did not know then what had happened anymore than the rest of the canines, but I saw Buddy standing behind the Labrador, his big head hanging, and I sensed he was in trouble. I left the other dogs to go to him. The dogs continued to whisper among themselves.

Sonny shot the pack a withering glance and a hush fell. "It's time. We have to cross."

"Can't I come along?" Badge asked.

"No, you may not."

Andy rose from his knee, stepped back, and saluted Badge.

Badge's head came up and he thrust his chest out. But I could see that his lip quivered, because the movement made his whiskers vibrate.

Sonny jumped over the wall into the creatureless void, his legs disappearing in the ground fog. The marine put a hip on the wall, swung his legs over, and followed. We could see that a group of humans had gathered to watch the spectacle. They peered over their wall as we were doing at ours.

When Sonny reached the middle of the empty featureless zone, he stopped. Andy turned back to see why the shepherd had halted, and then, understanding, marched on, alone.

# Chapter 34

I could not keep still. Waiting for Sonny to come back with the verdict was the worst sort of waiting. You know something awful is about to come down, but you can't help hoping for a break. A born cynic, I never expect to meet Lady Luck, but, somehow I kept imagining scenes where Sonny forgave Buddy, because Buddy is, well, so sweet.

Buddy stretched on the sand, his curly head resting on his paws. We were back in a desert, the cornfields had melted like butter in the sun, but there was something slapdash and dull about this new habitat, as if Sonny wasn't concentrating when he conjured it up.

"Here he comes." I saw the great white dog come over the dune, his paws sliding in the loose sand.

"He's not in much of a hurry." Buddy got up.

"That's not a good sign." I moved so that I was standing shoulder to shoulder with my friend.

Sonny approached and sat in front of Buddy. His amber eyes focused on the poodle, and they were as unreadable as the surface of a winter pond.

"Buddy, you have committed a grave wrong against your community."

"I know, and I am very sorry." Buddy's voice shook when he spoke.

"Everyone is angry. You have broken the Rule of Equi, and disturbed the balance," Sonny said. "You've made everyone afraid."

141

"But nothing has happened," I interrupted. "No earthquake. No hurricane."

"The powers wait to see if the punishment is just," Sonny said. "Buddy, you are hereby stripped of your wings and the privileges that go with them. You may no longer serve as guide."

"That's harsh. He was the best."

"I am not finished. You are exiled to the perimeter of Haven. You are to be shunned. Your fellow canines are not to speak to you."

I was angry. "That's not fair ..."

"What's fair, MacKenzie, fair for every dog, is restoring the balance."

A big tear slipped down Buddy's ski run of a nose and plopped onto the sand. "I have disgraced myself, Mac."

"I'll talk to you, Buddy. I'll go with you."

"You will do no such thing." Sonny walked up to me and thrust his face up to mine. "Buddy's sentence is open. His behavior will determine how long he is to be shunned. We will be watching. If you encourage him to break faith with his punishment, you will be responsible for prolonging his sentence."

"I brought this on myself, Mac," Buddy said. "I am ready for my punishment."

"Good, because your sentence begins immediately." Sonny flapped his wings once and lowered them to the sand. Buddy's wings slid off his back and settled on the ground. As we watched, they turned brittle, shattered into tiny fragments, and the wind took them away. "Now go."

We watched as Buddy trudged off toward the distant perimeter. His once proud dust mop of a tail, drooping like a ruined blossom broken at the stem.

# Chapter 35

Buddy made himself busy to fill the days. He tidied up the perimeter, stacking rocks into neat piles and dusting the wall with his tail. Sometimes, other residents of Haven would stroll along the perimeter, noting his cleanup work with appreciation, but no dog spoke to him, not once.

When I was not assigned to guide duty, I incorporated a sighting of Buddy into my daily routine. I would find a dune or knoll, depending on Sonny's environmental arrangements for the day, and sit where I could watch my friend from a safe distance. Howie and Skootch wanted to come, but they were too afraid of Sonny.

I could tell he knew I was watching. His pace would pick up and his tail would stand up straighter, but he did not acknowledge my presence in any outward fashion, like barking, wagging his tail, or prancing. I did not bark or wag either. I had taken Sonny's warning to heart, and I was not about to do anything that would lengthen Buddy's exile.

Even with his tidying and dusting, Buddy had a lot of time on his paws. He observed the activity over in the human section of Paradise Valley. People could often be seen walking arm in arm on the far side of the human wall, their heads bobbing along as they talked.

Buddy also learned that the creatureless void between the human and canine sections was not completely without character. If you were patient, the ground fog would shift and you could see boulders, stunted trees and ruts and ripples in the stony terrain. Once, Buddy even spotted a big log resting on the ground, but most of the time, the fog covered everything with a gray and chilly blanket.

One day, when he was particularly bored, Buddy decided to check out the void for himself. He had never seen any dog or human out there except for the awful day Sonny guided Andy to the human side, but what harm could there be?

Buddy looked around and saw no canines on his side or humans over the far wall. He jumped up on the wall and, hoping he wouldn't land on a big rock and sprain a paw, hopped into the fog. He stumbled a little because he could not see his footing, but all four of his paws landed square on the ground.

I'll just lie down in the fog if someone comes along and they won't see me, he thought. He worked his way to the middle of the zone. He found that if he concentrated he could see a few feet around and this made his progress easier.

Sometimes, the ground fell away, the fog became deeper, and his head sank into the mist , but most of the time, the layer was chest high. Buddy thought he would look pretty funny if anyone could have seen him, because his upper body would appear to float along the surface like a rubber ducky.

Buddy entered a deep section that was littered with huge boulders. As he wound his way through the rocks, he wished he had someone to play with. This spot was perfect for a game of hide and seek.

When he left the field of boulders, he was still in a deep portion, but he had meandered closer to the far side near the human wall. He looked up, saw a human on the wall and froze. Being under the fog was like being in the pool and seeing Leroy or Roxanne above, beyond the membrane of water. He could see the human, but from the person's vantage point, he was invisible.

It was a little girl, and she was walking along the wall with her arms outstretched to keep her balance. She was wearing cutoffs, a pink T-shirt, and matching pink baseball cap. Her sneakers had tiny pink lights that sparkled as she walked.

Buddy realized she could not see him for the fog. She was concentrating on her footing, and the tip of her tongue curled against her upper lip. She had big green eyes that reminded Buddy of Deedee's eyes. A lump formed in his throat and he looked at the little hands waving in the air like bird wings, and wondered how it would feel to have those hands caress the special place.

He wanted to go to the girl and introduce himself, but he was afraid he would startle her and she would fall. The wall was not that tall, but the girl was small and frail.

Buddy turned and trotted back toward the middle of the zone. He would wait until the girl tired of her tightrope game and sat down. He would reveal himself from the middle, a distance that should make her feel safe.

He did not have long to wait. The girl stopped at one of the periodic pillars that gave the wall its strength, sat and dangled her sneakers into the fog as if she were sitting by a stream splashing her toes in the water.

Buddy cleared his throat and barked his best welcome bark. The girl jumped at the sound, but spotted him and smiled. Encouraged, Buddy approached her.

When he reached the wall, the girl leaned down and patted his topknot. "What a big dog! I've never seen anything so big!"

Buddy put his front paws up on the wall so she could see how tall he really was.

"Our next door neighbor had an English Setter, but you are much bigger than Nigel."

The girl moved her hand to Buddy's neck, stroking his muscles with a gentle touch. His eyes closed with the pleasure of it.

145

"My parents wouldn't let us have a dog. My sister, Linda, is allergic to just about everything."

The girl's hand slid to the special place and scratched. Buddy thought he would melt like snow on a sunny day.

"Of course, when I learned I had cancer, I realized it was better I didn't have a pet. All those trips to the hospital. There were the therapy dogs, but I don't think they let you bring your own dog into the ward."

Buddy jumped up on the wall and sat next to the girl.

"My name is Gwen," she said. "I used to have red hair, so I didn't wear pink much although it's my favorite color. So, now that I'm bald, I can wear it as much as I like."

Gwen pulled her cap off and showed Buddy her shiny head. Buddy leaned over and licked her behind the ear, wondering if humans had a special place.

Gwen giggled. "That tickles." She threw her thin arms around Buddy and hugged him. "I can feel your heart beating," Gwen said, hugging him harder. "There are some kids here, but not so many. Besides, I'd rather play with you."

Buddy could feel her warm breath on his chest. He ached to be of use again. This was the first time since the loss of his guide privileges that he felt like he had a purpose. If he could make this little girl happy, it would be something. I'll be your dog, he thought. I'll be the pet you never had.

When I came to the dune that day, Buddy was nowhere in sight. Puzzled, I sat and scanned the horizon. A movement in the creatureless void caught my attention. The fog rolled as if something was moving underneath. As I watched, Buddy shot out of the gray soup, landed on the wall, and jumped down into Haven. Even from a distance I could see that his eyes were bright and there was a spring in his step I had not seen in a long time.

146

I knew my friend was breaking the Rule of Equi again just as surely as I knew my name was MacKenzie, and I recognized I could not help him. I could not talk to him and make him see reason. I could not wrestle him to the ground and keep him from going over the wall and further jeopardizing his already precarious situation. I shook and snorted in frustration. Never had I felt so helpless, not even when I was up against the Hummer.

# Chapter 36

It was inevitable, of course. I was not the only dog that came to observe Buddy. True to his word, Sonny visited now and then to gauge Buddy's compliance with his sentence. When Sonny appeared, I would slink off my dune and retreat to a stand of trees or a rock formation, whatever was available. I did not want to draw attention to my vigil or in any way cause Sonny to question Buddy's or my adherence to the rules.

Sonny arrived, and although I had no other choice but to run and hide behind a cluster of cactuses, I was frantic. Not a half hour before, I had seen Buddy jump the canine wall, collect the girl, and take her to play hide and seek among the boulders, a favorite pastime of theirs.

Sonny scanned the scene looking for Buddy. I prayed the dog and the child would not reappear. My prayers were not answered. Buddy's head emerged from the fog pointed in the direction of the human wall. Next, the girl's head became visible, her pink cap bobbing along beside the big dog, her arm draped over his shoulders. When the two reached the human's wall, the girl climbed on Buddy's back to reach the top.

Sonny's face darkened with anger. His ears came to rigid points. I knew he was thinking that the familiar actions of the dog and the girl meant this was no chance encounter. Buddy was not only guilty of being in the creatureless void, he was doing the unthinkable, fraternizing with a human.

What would become of my friend? What would they do to him? Buddy's current punishment was the most severe anyone in Haven could remember.

Sonny approached the canine wall and sat in its shade to wait.

Buddy left the girl and bounded across the creatureless void. His passing caused the fog to swirl in angry little tornadoes. Smiling happily, tongue and ears bouncing, Buddy sailed over the wall back into Haven like a horse at a steeplechase.

"Welcome back," Sonny said.

Buddy spun and came face-to-face with the shepherd.

"What have you been up to?"

Buddy gulped. "I've been playing with a little girl. She was never allowed to have a pet, so I'm sort of standing in."

"Standing in for a pet. A position that is forbidden in Haven." Sonny rose to his full height. "Haven dogs are subservient to no one."

"I know, but she seemed so lonely. I wanted to help her."

"You have broken the Rule for a second time. This is unprecedented. It will go badly for you, Buddy. Come with me." Sonny turned and saw me. "Mac, you bring up the rear."

The three of us trudged down toward the center of Haven. As we progressed, we acquired more and more spectators. At first the crowd simply followed, whispering. Quickly, however, the dogs concluded that Buddy's return from the perimeter under guard could mean only one thing—he had done something awful. Faces became angry, teeth bared. Whispering turned to irate barking and harsh growling.

By the time we reached the center of the community, the crowd had turned into a mob.

Sonny stopped in front of a row of kennels and pushed open the door to the middle one. The kennels were large as automobiles, and although they were shaped like travel carriers, were built of stone. "You'll be safer here."

Head drooping so low his nose almost touched the ground, Buddy entered the cell. Sonny nosed the door closed.

He might be safe from the unruly mob, but he would be the object of ridicule day and night. Maybe that was part of Sonny's plan. I glared at the shepherd, no longer caring if he read my thoughts.

Sonny did not blink. "I am going to the mountains. I wish to consult my own thoughts and confer with other elders."

The sky grew dark, and it began to rain. I hoped the weather was just a reflection of Sonny's mood, and not caused by an imbalance in our paradise brought about by my friend's actions. The rain did help disperse the crowd. Dogs hurried away in twos and threes. From their expressions, I concluded they thought Haven was in trouble.

# Chapter 37

 Howie licked his coat three more times to get his fur to settle down. He was so hyped up, his golden feathers seemed to be going every which way at once.

I checked my paws again. I wanted to make a good impression. "So, Sonny opted for a court to assure balance is restored."

"And, if it isn't, it won't be his fault alone. Even though this has started among the canines, we'll be able to share the blame." Howie held his tail out for Skootch to inspect.

"It looks fine, Howie," Skootch said. "Sonny is smart to kick the whole thing upstairs."

I thought it was devious, but, then, I had always hated political maneuvering. I was a woman of action. "Tell me again about the players."

"Judges. Honorable judges. The Communal Tribunal is comprised of learned representatives for the major communities in Paradise Valley. Bjorn will represent us."

Skootch nodded. "Another stroke of genius on Sonny's part. Rather than sitting on the court, he will prosecute Buddy. Looks more even-pawed that way."

"Think of it as good guy, bad guy," Howie said. "Sonny can come across tough as nails. And Bjorn, that big hulk of a Great Dane, looks formidable, but he has the heart of an Easter Bunny."

"Got it. What about the rest of the line up?" If I were going to lead the defense team, I had to know what made these judges tick.

"Hephzibah the Hierophant is the high priestess of the felines. She will represent the rest of the animals, another inspired choice, because everyone knows dogs and cats have issues," Howie said, rubbing his ears. "Holy Oak is representing the plant kingdom, and Minerva Goldbrick is representing the elements."

I watched as the judges filed into place at the long table that had been positioned at the north end of Haven's central square. "And Old Solomon represents the humans and is the chief justice."

"Right," Howie said. "I'm not entirely sure what Sonny's thinking was on letting the human be the chief justice. Buddy's offense involved a human."

"I think it works," Skootch said. "Look at the guy. With those jowls and that barrel chest he looks like a Basset Hound."

I saw Sonny approaching. He signaled two Doberman Pinschers to collect Buddy from the kennel. I thought the guards were overkill. Buddy would never cause trouble in a situation like this.

I checked my appearance one last time. "Now you guys let me know somehow if you think I'm off track. I'm kinda winging it, but my main strategy is to focus on Buddy's goodness."

"We've got your back," Howie said. "I'll clear my throat if I think we need to confer."

The three of us moved to the defense table. Sonny was on our right. The Dobermans escorted Buddy to a platform in the middle facing the judges. The rest of the square was packed with canines. Smaller dogs struggled toward the front so they could see. I thought of Javier and wished he could be here to help me fight for Buddy. Skootch and Howie were great, but they were pretty laid back compared to that fiery Latino.

Sonny greeted the judge, nodded to me and began his argument. "At the time of his most recent offense, Buddy, the

Standard Poodle, was already serving a sentence for breaking the Rule of Equi—"

"Objection." I hurried in front of our table. "We are not here to try Buddy for past offenses. Sonny should not be allowed to go over old ground."

"I am merely establishing the circumstances that put Buddy at the perimeter where he had the opportunity to go over the wall and talk to the human girl," Sonny said.

"Sounds reasonable. Overruled," Old Solomon said.

Sheepish, I returned to my table. Skootch rubbed against my shoulder.

Sonny continued to make his case, telling the story of Badge and the young marine. I looked around to see if I could spot Badge. If he were here, I could call on him. He would be a good character witness. I whispered to Howie, "See if you can find Badge, but don't be gone too long."

Howie nodded and slipped into the crowd behind us.

Sonny had moved on to Buddy's encounter with the girl. "Despite the fact that Buddy received a thorough orientation like every dog who comes to Haven, and that the importance of the Rule of Equi was reinforced at the time of his sentencing for his previous offense, he committed a flagrant violation of the rule again."

Sonny paused to let his remarks sink in. He was making Buddy sound willful, painting him as a dog who had no regard for other canines.

"Unlike his first offense, where it could be argued that he was in a tough spot, and had to make a snap decision, Buddy was under no pressure this time. He entered the creatureless void because he was bored. Bored!"

Again Sonny paused and paced across in front of the judges. The cat and the oak were nodding. I could not read Minerva's expression, because the sun was shining on her gleaming surface, but Old Solomon's jowls dipped in agreement.

Sonny stopped right in front of Buddy. "Now we get to the worst part. He meets the little girl, and he is nice to her. Although that is breaking the rule, I am sure many of you here can sympathize with a dog who hears about a child's battle with cancer. Dogs get cancer too. But Buddy didn't just listen. Buddy decided to be her pet. He decided to put himself into a subservient position on purpose!"

Gasps came from the crowd. Although everyone already knew the story, Sonny's retelling of it was so dramatic, it was like hearing the tale for the very first time. My paw-and-a-prayer defense of Buddy was not going to prevail against this masterful performance. I scanned the crowd for Howie.

"Now we get to central horror of this whole sorry affair." Sonny stepped forward so that he was almost in Buddy's face. "Buddy didn't break the Rule of Equi once, like he did the other time. He broke it daily! He jumped the wall and met the girl and played with her every day. Played with her like a pet." He spat the word out like it had a bad taste.

Growls of outrage punctuated the silence, as Sonny walked back to his table. "The prosecution rests."

Several dogs came forward carrying pails of water. The pails were placed in front of each of the judges. Water also was delivered to Sonny and to our table. Sonny lapped from his pail, indulging in a long, satisfying drink.

Howie popped out of the crowd next to Sonny's table and trotted over to me. "No sign of Badge," he said.

My heart sank. I had nothing to work with. I was going to fail Buddy. Horrible rumors about the nature of Buddy's punishment were circulating. Because no one could remember a case like this, a dog didn't know what to believe, but one awful possibility had captured the imagination of many dogs—that Buddy would be taken to the mountains and walled up in a cave, never to see light, or hear a happy bark, or receive a friendly lick. I shivered.

"MacKenzie, I believe it is time for you to speak," Old Solomon said.

I walked toward the judges. As I passed Buddy, I tried to smile at him, but my lip quivered. He smiled his big, dopey grin, and I knew he was putting all his faith in me. I felt like I had fallen in an icy river.

"Honorable judges, my friend Buddy is a good dog. The best. Until the unfortunate misunderstanding about the Afghanistan mission, he was thought to be among the very best of the guides. I am sure there are many dogs here who can tell you how they were brought to Haven with gentleness and sensitivity."

"Buddy's talents aren't an issue here," Sonny interrupted.

"Yes, MacKenzie, we know Buddy is a sweetie," Hephzibah said. "I think you can move on." The way the cat said "sweetie," made it sound like a rattler hissing.

"My point is that Buddy is all about goodness. He tries to be a good friend, a good citizen, and a good guide. His intentions are pure."

"So he's good as gold," Minerva said, drawing a chuckle from the crowd. "But he did something bad."

"Did he?" I approached her. "I don't think the Rule of Equi works like a big set of scales. I don't believe that an act of spontaneous goodness can be placed on the evil side of the scale and make the scale go down. The goodness would rise up like a golden cloud." It was a risk talking to Minerva about scales, since she knew a lot about weights and measures, but I felt for the first time since I had been talking that I was onto something. Before she had looked smug, now, she looked confused.

I moved down the row to the cat. "The Rule of Equi is not black and white either. Something is either this or it is that. I don't believe that for a minute." I smiled at her. "Cats purr. Nobody knows what purring is exactly, do they, priestess?"

"Well, no. We just know that to purr is to be." Her yellow eyes winked.

"Exactly. It is the feline mantra. The mysterious, glorious symphony of the cat kingdom. How could anything so beautiful and pleasurable be reduced to black and white?"

"Never." Hephzibah's whiskers vibrated with passion.

I moved to the Great Dane. "Judge Bjorn, the Rule of Equi is all about balance, right?"

"Of course." The big dog said, his paws crossed before him on the table.

"When something is in balance, that is good, and when something is out of balance, that is bad?"

Bjorn nodded in agreement.

"I have heard that you are one of the best cookie jugglers in Haven. You can balance a cookie on your nose for the longest time. Longer than anyone."

Bjorn was flattered. "It is a talent of mine."

"How do you know the cookie is in balance? How do you do it?

"I just do. I can't explain it."

"Kind of like purring," I said. "The way we know if you are successful or not is by the consequences."

"Yes, if I fail, the cookie falls off my nose and breaks."

"So out of balance equals broken cookie?"

"Of course, that almost never happens with my cookies," Bjorn said, "but, yes, you are right."

"What I want to know about what Buddy did is this: Where is the broken cookie?" I paced along the line of judges, looking into each face.

"Where are the evil consequences of Buddy's act?" Now I walked along the edge of the crowd. "Some dogs have said that the rain we had the day Buddy was put in the kennel was a sign."

Many dogs in the crowd nodded. Especially, the smaller ones. I kept my voice even. "I like rain. Maybe it is because I am a desert dog, but I love to run in the rain. What about you, Judge Bjorn?"

"Running in the rain is good."

I returned to the judge's table and stood before the oak tree. There was a lot of debris around the great tree, shriveled leaves and broken twigs, but the oak was so revered, no one dared call attention to it. "Judge Holy Oak, I believe the Rule of Equi can be improved."

"Young woman, you are impudent to suggest such a thing."

"Let me explain my meaning. The rule is like a garden. If the garden is tended, there is more fruit and more beautiful flowers. It is still the garden, but it has grown."

The oak dipped his bows in one majestic nod.

"So if you put more goodness in, the rule is magnified. Kind of like you. You started out as a little acorn, but look at you now. You are the same, yet there is so much more of you."

I walked along the perimeter of the shadow the enormous tree threw on the ground to emphasize just how big Holy Oak was.

"Buddy's good act didn't unbalance the rule, it made the rule stronger, broader, bigger."

I stepped toward Old Solomon. The wise old human cocked a brow and studied me as he drummed his fingers on the table. He had a nose like Kurtz's. I sensed that he was not buying my performance. So far, ideas had come to me as I progressed down the table. Now, my mind went blank.

Behind me, Howie cleared his throat. I turned and looked at him. He was smiling and jerking his head to the left. I looked in that direction.

Badge was fighting his way toward the front. Wading through the crowd of dogs behind him were Andy and the little girl. The marine held the child's hand.

I inhaled a chest full of air. I could call Badge to speak on Buddy's behalf. Surely, Old Solomon would find Badge's testimony persuasive.

I watched the faces of the dogs as the humans passed by. Many dogs looked longingly at the humans, like they were finding something they'd mislaid or seeing something they'd missed. No, it wasn't Badge, it was about the humans. Something humans had.

Andy picked up the little girl and lifted her over the row of small dogs at the front of the assembly, her feet dangling between a Welsh Corgie and a Kerri Blue Terrier. He set the child on her feet in the open space between the defense and the prosecution tables.

Gwen smiled at the marine and then at Buddy. She dropped Andy's hand and gave Buddy a salute.

I turned to Old Solomon. "The Rule of Equi is about balancing. Balancing important things, not cookies. Buddy wasn't unbalancing the rule when he chose to guide the marine or befriend the girl, he was rebalancing it."

"How could that be so?" The chief justice leaned forward, showing real interest in my reasoning for the first time.

"When Buddy died, he gave up his role of subservience to humans, just as all dogs do. But he got something too. He got free will, the thing humans have. That is what Equi means. We are equal with humans. When Buddy chose to be the girl's friend, he was exercising his free will."

I turned around to face the crowd. I was looking right at Sonny and he was looking right at me.

I looked back at Sonny without blinking. "You see, there was no subservience in Buddy's heart, only caring."

The shepherd's eyes were filled with respect.

"The defense rests."

The communal tribunal did not take long to return a verdict. Even the Dobermans barked approval as Buddy was set free, and they are a breed not known for spontaneous outbursts of gaiety.

Buddy hugged me and gave me a big, juicy lick across the jowls. "Mac, you were awesome. I thought I was a goner."

"We thought you were a goner, too," Howie said, washing Buddy's ear.

"Well, thanks a lot!" I said. "That was not exactly a vote of confidence."

"He means we're a bunch of amateurs," Skootch said. "But you had enough passion to win. That's the important thing."

Sonny walked up to Buddy, and we all went silent. "Congratulations, Buddy. No hard feelings, I hope. Just doing my job."

"I understand, Sonny. When do you think I can have my wings back?"

Sonny grinned and blinked hard. Buddy's wings materialized and the poodle almost fell over from the unexpected weight.

"Gee, thanks, Sonny!"

"No problem. Just promise me one thing. Try to stay out of trouble for a while, so I don't have to face Mac in court any time soon."

We all chuckled at that, and Sonny came over and licked me on the forehead.

"Order, order," the chief justice shouted. "Our panel has something further to say."

The crowd, which had been breaking up, reversed and pressed forward. We turned and faced the judges.

Old Solomon rose and smoothed his robes. "The other judges and I believe that Buddy deserves a reward for time served, something that goes beyond having his reputation restored, getting his wings back and being allowed to return to guide duty. We are going to give Buddy a guide assignment this very day, an assignment that is unprecedented."

Solomon spread his arms before the crowd. "We believe that significant inter-community progress has been made here today. In view of this, we have decided to try a new approach, a little experiment."

"He means we're going to turn over a new leaf," Holy Oak said.

Old Solomon smiled. "Buddy, you will be the first dog ever assigned to guide a human to Paradise Valley."

The crowd gasped. We looked at each other, speechless. Buddy looked like he had been turned into an alabaster statue.

"Of course, you don't have to accept the mission. You can exercise your free will and refuse." The chief justice shot me a look of mock seriousness, before turning to Buddy. "The name of the human is Deedee Holmes."

# Chapter 38

 On his way to Yucca Dunes, Buddy caught up with Holy Oak near the perimeter. The great tree moved slowly because of all its heavy boughs and lengthy root system, which trailed along behind the oak like a king's royal train.

The dog greeted the ancient tree and thanked him again for participating in the tribunal. As he turned to go, the tree spoke.

"Wait, Buddy. Come closer. I have one more gift for you. Something that will forever remind you of this day. When you are happy, it will remind everyone of what a special dog you are."

Buddy came to the oak and stepped into the shade of its boughs. Two of the limbs nearest the ground waved above his head and a fine dust drifted down from the leaves, coating his fur.

"There, I think that should do it. Now, be on your way."

"Thank you, again, sir." Mystified, Buddy trotted to the perimeter of Haven, and started to dematerialize. The dust had a pleasant smell, like the flowers in Deedee's garden.

He concentrated hard on the garden, and when he opened his eyes he was there. It was night and the surface of the pool twinkled as the soft wind moved the water. The sound of leaves skittering across the tiles was the only noise.

Entering the house through the dog door brought back so many memories. He could have passed through the wall, but it seemed more respectful to come in this way.

When he came to Deedee's bedroom, his big heart almost burst with the joy of reunion. Deedee lay on her big sleigh bed, her gray head on a pink pillow. Maxine and Eliza sat on either side of her, each holding her hand. Leroy and Roxanne sat at the foot of the bed. Leroy's head rested on his two front paws, which were pressed down on the quilt just so, the doggie position for praying.

Buddy touched his nose against Roxanne's cheek and inhaled her sweet, subtle diversity aroma. Of course she could not see or feel him. None of them could, but that did not lessen his pleasure at being with his family again.

He eased closer and watched Deedee. She was breathing, but the breaths were very shallow.

Buddy said her name over and over in his head. Deedee. Deedee. Deedee. I love you, Deedee.

On the bed, Deedee whispered, "Bud."

Maxine leaned forward. "Mom?"

Deedee's soul eased itself free, like shrugging off a coat. She rose and floated at the edge of the bed, where she could watch the scene.

Maxine put her face next to her mother's. "She's gone, Eliza," she said, and started to sob.

Eliza took the hand she was holding and placed it on her aunt's breast. She put her free hand on her cousin's shaking shoulder, tears sliding down her own cheeks.

Deedee turned and saw Buddy for the first time. "Buddy. I should have known you would come."

As she floated to his side, Buddy's soul did a summersault. When she knelt in front of him and rubbed the special place, his heart beat a skiptoomaloo.

"I am your Buddy. I love you just as much as ever. Although we've been apart, nothing can change that."

"Well, something has certainly changed," Deedee said, pointing to his tail.

Buddy turned and looked at his tail. It wasn't white anymore. There was white, but also blue and red and green and yellow. All those dust particles that had fallen from the boughs of the great oak had migrated to his tail and turned into gold and silver sparkles.

"That is the happiest tail that ever was," Deedee said, clapping her hands in delight.

"Did you see that?" Roxanne asked Leroy.

Leroy rubbed his paw over his eyes. "I saw something."

Deedee rose. "That bouquet on your bottom is causing a stir."

"We had better go." Buddy turned, and a rainbow of tiny lights danced in his wake.

"Hold onto my topknot."

Deedee threaded her fingers in Buddy's fur, and off they went on their history-making journey to Paradise Valley, a place made even more perfect by the good thoughts and brave deeds of Buddy Boutonniere.

# Chapter 39

 So, that's what became of the dog who broke the biggest rule of all. He went from being a swell guy with a silly tail who survived tragic circumstances, to the best hot diggidy guide in the universe. His cosmic corsage of a tail is the delight of every creature in Paradise Valley and the object of a great deal of envy among the guides, I don't mind telling you. Canines gather around when he's coming in from a mission, just to watch Buddy make a landing.

Javier and Derek are with us now. Derek's memory has returned and his feet have been restored to their proper color. He much prefers guide work to guarding kitty poop. Happily, the wing thing has relieved Javier of the need to be afraid of feet. Skootch and Buddy often sit by the ebony pool and watch Leroy and Roxanne far below giving the roof rats a little exercise. Their time is far in the future, and, besides, Maxine needs them.

As for me, I am at last at peace. Oh, I will never be a quiet dog, patient and still. I channel those energies into running with the wind until I become crystals, and singing my song loud and true so it echoes from the mountains. And, of course, like Buddy, I work on being the best guide I can be.

I am at peace, because Buddy's journey taught me that I cannot save every dog. Not me, little Miss Fix-It MacKenzie. What I can do is be part of something bigger than me. I realize now, that my mission is to save one dog at a time. It is the same mission given to each and every one of us.

# Acknowledgements

I would like to thank Sally Willis Rogers, Dale Johnson, Ron Ruelle, Ron's daughter, Lillian, and Susan Friedlund for assisting with this project with their time, talent, hard work, wisdom, and enthusiasm.

I also am indebted to a beta team of Coachella Valley mom and kid reviewers. I'll bet you young folks were surprised when you found out an unpublished manuscript was part of your curriculum! I hope that in addition to developing a book that pleases readers, I also have inspired a writer or two. Thank you, Alexis Stefani, Martin Stefani, Lynda Stefani, Jillian Wilcox, Brooke Wilcox, Aaron Wilcox and Jeannette Wilcox.

Finally, I want to thank my parents for introducing me to life on a farm, where I was privileged to grow up in the company of many noble creatures, among them my first canine pals, Scupper, Susie Q and Beauregard. Mom and Dad also introduced me to the world of books. The farm may be gone, and my first pooches are in Haven, but my happy memories persist, and the books live forever.

Out of respect for the dogs who inspired this story, I have chosen to capitalize breed names. I also have capitalized the one cat breed mentioned; although cats play a minor role in this tale, you know how finicky they are. For my 'supporting cast' of birds, small animals, plants and trees, I have chosen common names and presented them in lower case. The raven who lives in the palm tree in our backyard already has lodged an objection.

K. Anne Russell
Palm Desert CA
March 2011
russell@rwwra.com

# Buddy's Tail Web Site

Teachers and parents can find instructional materials, and kids can find fun stuff at http://www.buddystail.com.

Made in the USA
Las Vegas, NV
24 January 2022

42185561R00098